Chapter 1

I was invited to a Skype interview with Maren Rand, an Editor in Chief of Brandon House Publishing in New York for a position as a cultural events columnist. What had originally been scheduled as a one hour casual conversation had turned into months' worth of religiously appointed story-telling sessions.

I must admit that I wasn't completely truthful with Maren at first. As time went on however, I was no longer able to help myself.

MAREN: What word do you hate to use the most and why?

JAIMEY: Love, because it's so ridiculously overused that it's lost its meaning.

MAREN: Here's an off topic question: have you ever been . . . well . . . let me rephrase that. Have you ever experienced that 'lost meaning'?

JAIMEY: I think so. No. Well, I don't know. Maybe. I don't know.

MAREN: Let's try to make sense of this confusion shall we? Expand on it. I'd like to hear how good a commentary you can be. And I'll have none of

	that crap about 'I love art and my mom.' Give me the good stuff.
JAIMEY:	Well, there are many confusing tales revolving around that subject matter. I've never really reflected on them long enough to make sense of them. Whatever happened, happened. Who cares, you know?
MAREN:	Fair enough. Let's reflect. Tell me the story of your first one.
JAIMEY:	It's not really much of a story. I really didn't even know the person. I'd been in other relationships before. But in all of them, I'd always kept my . . . .
MAREN:	Your what?
JAIMEY:	I don't know how to describe it.
MAREN:	Try
JAIMEY:	It was as if I was a ghost. I would force my consciousness to break away from my body to escape the experience. And I'd float above myself and whomever it was that I was involved with at the time and observe what was happening, in this utterly utopic feeling of relief.
MAREN:	Wow, they must have been bad lovers.

JAIMEY: Physically? No. I dated eye candies. And come to think of it, they were all quite the sensitive individuals. I suppose it was just me. I never allowed myself to reciprocate. I mean I liked them. But love? I don't know. Ugh. Did I just say the word? I did, didn't I? See, I even HATE saying it. It means nothing. It has no substance left.

Anyway, because I never expressed my acknowledgement to their feelings towards me, they simply grew cold and eventually broke it off.

MAREN: What made you even have these relationships then?

JAIMEY: What do you mean?

MAREN: You seem like the kind of person who is in touch with your feelings. Am I correct? I mean, you are a writer. Most writers are. But if you numb yourself from affection and intimacy, why even do it?

JAIMEY: Good question. I suppose the best answer is simply that I wanted to feel normal—in the beginning, at least. I'd grown up thinking that it was the thing to do. You go to school, make friends, go to college, work; somewhere in the middle, you meet someone interested in you and you get married, have kids, retire and die.

MAREN: Your voice turned into a monotone just now. That's interesting. So, who was the guy?

JAIMEY: What? Is it that obvious?

MAREN: I'm a woman. I know. Tell me about him. Wait. What time is it? I have to go but what's your schedule like tomorrow? I'd like to call you back on a second interview. And then you can tell me about him.

JAIMEY: Great! How about the same time?

MAREN: Yes, that's perfect. Well, Jaimey I'm very excited about this so far. Keep it going. You may have a place with us, yet.

JAIMEY: Thank you. I'll talk to you tomorrow, Maren.

MAREN: Bye, Bye.

Chapter 2

I was getting a bit skeptical about this whole scenario. If she did indeed want to see how I was with commentary, wasn't what I'd told her yesterday enough? Why would anyone be interested in my boring love life? I went along with it, however. I hated the subject that she'd brought up so I tried to cut it short by brushing it off as unimportant. Besides, how the hell am I supposed to know what love is? I'm single: didn't that say something? Still, I kept at it to keep her satisfied. I'd have killed for this job.

MAREN: Yes, so where were we? Ah! You were going to tell me about the guy who made you numb to the world.

JAIMEY: I wasn't numb to the world-just relationships-just love. It's Cliché. I wasn't ever in love. I was in . . . cliché.

MAREN: What else is there though, but love?

JAIMEY: Really? You don't know?

MAREN: Oh I know there are a lot in hindsight. But you're so young. There shouldn't be anything else.

JAIMEY: You'd be surprised. In fact, quite possibly the main reason why I felt the need to stay at an arm's length away from everyone was because I wanted freedom.

MAREN: What were you a prisoner to?

JAIMEY: Tradition. I was born and bred as the Asian stepford wife. And after college, I was ripe for the picking. Suitors would schedule appointments with my parents to come and see me for an interview. I'd cook them dinner to show that I'd be capable to feed my husband and our kids. My mom would dress me up in all my fineries and hang her jewelries all over my body as if I it was a store front display case.

MAREN: You're talking about arranged marriage.

JAIMEY: Yes. I had a designated husband at 8.

MAREN: So why the suitors?

JAIMEY: He didn't like what he saw when he came over so the parents backed off.

MAREN: Harsh.

JAIMEY: Not really. I kinda' had a hand in it. I'd made up some bullshit about me being pregnant to make him not like me. And I'm relieved that it worked. I didn't want to get married at all. This husband thing had been looming over my head like a dark cloud ever since I could remember. My entire life was focused on it. I couldn't breathe.

MAREN: I see why freedom is so important to you.

JAIMEY: Indeed, it has always been the driving force.

MAREN: So back to this guy . . .

JAIMEY: Gabriel.

MAREN: Tell me about him.

JAIMEY: We'd grown up together. I was a sheltered child. I couldn't date. Hell, my dad wouldn't let me watch Disney movies that involved kissing. They'd let me hang out with Gabe because his parents were very close friends with my mom. In fact, when they'd finally moved to America in the late 90's, they came to live with us. My parents rented one of the extra bedrooms to them. Gabe would come every year or so for a visit but he went to school in the Philippines. And every summer, we would have month-long vacations back there.

Gabe and I were inseparable. Of course being so young, we didn't realize what was brewing. In fact, it wasn't until around the beginning of high school that things heated up.

MAREN: How did it start?

JAIMEY: It's a bit blurry now. But whatever happened, I knew that he was sincere. His intentions with me were honest and . . . well, it was something that I knew . . . I . . . know for a fact, was real.

MAREN: How are you so sure?

JAIMEY: He was hot. I was fat and ugly. And it didn't matter.

MAREN: Wow. Umm . . . Okay. But a lot of men like curvy women.

JAIMEY: I was a girl. My parents wouldn't even let me wear makeup. No. Whatever he saw in me was something truly genuine.

MAREN: So what was the problem?

JAIMEY: I wouldn't have sex with him. I wanted to hold it off until after marriage.

MAREN: You were a virgin?

JAIMEY: ummm . . .

MAREN: Sorry. Don't answer that if you don't want to.

JAIMEY: Anyway, he's two years older than me and the Philippines didn't have such a thing as Jr. High so by the time I was a sophomore in high school, he was already a freshman in college. It was getting more and more difficult to see him. We'd talk on the phone for hours almost every day, though. I'd tell him, everything. He was one of the very few people who took my goals seriously. He encouraged me to keep focus on school so that I'd have something to fall back on when I finally rounded up the courage to leave home. I believed that this was why he respected my choice in waiting.

MAREN: Did you love him?

JAIMEY: I wanted to marry him.

MAREN: That wasn't my question.

JAIMEY: I don't know that I knew what it meant. It hurt a lot when we ended it-especially since I'd constantly have to see him in family gatherings and soirées. Following that year when we'd broken up, I began to lose weight. He'd notice me more and more and would apologize to me each time we had a moment alone together.

MAREN: Why did you break up?

JAIMEY: He'd gotten a girl pregnant in the Philippines.

MAREN: Ouch.

JAIMEY: He'd kept it from me for nine months.

MAREN: How long were you an item?

JAIMEY: Almost 5 years. I think I handled it very well. I hid everything of course. My clan is famous for sweeping things under the rug. I stood firm and told him that I didn't ever want to see him again. He has a child now and his focus must be on his family.

MAREN: So, he still wanted to be with you.

JAIMEY: Yes. At least, that's what he said. And he was persistent too. Shortly after all this had happened, my family and I went back home on our yearly trips. I'd called ahead and asked him to stay away. By this time, he'd been trying to get a hold of me like there was no tomorrow. The phones were ringing off the hook and every other day, I'd receive flowers or some sort of gift at my door. But I couldn't talk to him. I could barely speak. I didn't know how to react.

MAREN: Did anything happen when you went back?

JAIMEY: Oh yes, and did it ever! I still have the scar to prove it.

MAREN: What? Whoa. What happened?

JAIMEY: Like I said, I didn't know how to express my feelings towards what had happened. And one afternoon, I was walking past the window outside and saw him standing in the living room with a bouquet of flowers. This was when all hell broke loose. I still have no idea where my strength and reasoning came from.

MAREN: What happened?

JAIMEY: I punched the window in. He wasn't even anywhere near it, but I punched it towards his direction. My hand was bleeding so much that they had to take me to the emergency room and perform a minor surgery because they couldn't pull out all of the glass from my knuckles.

MAREN: Oh my. How did he react?

JAIMEY: I hadn't noticed. I passed out. He didn't speak to me until about a month later when his family attended our annual summer party. We'd throw this huge celebration for the barrio people before returning to the states. I didn't think he'd come, but I was glad in the end. I think it was the day that I'd forced myself to forgive him.

MAREN: What made that day different from the others?

JAIMEY: It was the day that I saw his little girl.

MAREN: What about her made you forgive him?

JAIMEY: She was so precious. She had his eyes. I had to keep composure in public so I had to pretend to be interested in the addition to his family. When they handed her to me, that was it.

Don't misunderstand my not wanting to marry for not wanting a family. I'd always wanted a family of my own. I'd always wanted a child. And I'd always imagined my child coming from him.

Anyway, from the moment I saw her, all was forgiven. I loved her like I was her mother. At that moment, I wanted nothing but the best for her. Gabriel, regardless of his cheating ways was a good man in every other aspect. I knew that he'd make a good dad. And this brought my soul to peace.

MAREN: That's beautiful.

JAIMEY: So how about that job offer?

MAREN: Well you see here's the thing: Since your background is in Business, and the position is more geared to individuals with journalism majors, I'd have to speak with my superiors and get back to you. Are you free next Monday around this time?

JAIMEY: Yes, that's not a problem. Thank you for your support. I really want this job.

MAREN: Well, I personally am very confident in your abilities. Unfortunately, it's not me who'll be cutting your checks. So I'll see you on Monday then?

JAIMEY: Monday.

Chapter 3

MAREN: Jaimey, I have to tell you the truth. I really like you. Your story is something I'd avidly read if it were a book and I must confess, that's why I've prolonged our interviews. But as far as the job, I'm afraid it's already been offered to someone with a journalism background. Please don't be too upset. I'd like to keep going. I want to collaborate with you somehow on a possible book.

JAIMEY: I need a job. If it were to work out, I'd need something on the side.

MAREN: I understand, completely. I suppose I'm asking for forgiveness because I didn't tell you sooner. But I do believe, wholeheartedly that you've got the makings of a really good book here.

JAIMEY: I appreciate that. I guess.

MAREN: I understand your disappointment but I do want you to know how grateful I am that you're willing to move forward with this.

JAIMEY: It's something to do, I suppose. It'll keep my mind off the stress of job and house hunting.

MAREN: Yes, it's been a while since we'd spoken. Are you in New York now?

JAIMEY: Yes. I got here last Saturday.

MAREN: It must have been hard, leaving London. I know how much you loved the place.

JAIMEY: Yeah, it was rather difficult. But to tell you the truth, now that I'm here I'm very excited. Everything that needed closure back in London got its due. I'm back to being me. And I've scored a bunch of writing gigs in the week that I'd been here so things are looking up.

MAREN: That sounds amazing! I'm happy for you. Now what do you say about my offer? This can just be another side gig. And now that you're in NY, we can meet up in person. You really have nothing to lose, and pardon the cliché but, everything to gain.

JAIMEY: I don't forgive you for that. I hate clichés. It's the same idea that our meetings revolve around.

MAREN: Wait . . . was that a yes?

JAIMEY: Okay. But the third one, I'm a bit hesitant about. It's fresh. Wait . . . maybe this was the fourth one.

MAREN: Maybe?

JAIMEY: Well, the official second one was a bit complicated

MAREN: How so?

JAIMEY: First off . . . well wait . . . maybe I'm not ready to tell you.

MAREN: That bad?

JAIMEY: Yeah it's really twisted. At the time, I thought I loved her.

MAREN: Her?

JAIMEY: Yeah. But that's not the twisted part.

MAREN: Of course not. But what was it?

JAIMEY: I'm not ready. Maybe if I tell you about the third one . . . . She's also a 'her.'

MAREN: Hold on, forgive me but when will you be ready to talk about the second one?

JAIMEY: I don't know if it applies. It's twisted because I wasn't meant to have feelings like that towards her.

MAREN: Because she was a she?

JAIMEY: No. Because . . . . well it didn't have anything to do with her sexuality-wait . . . maybe. I don't know. I just haven't figured it out yet. I don't want to deal with it. I'm not ready.

MAREN: Okay. Maybe we can get back to it after you tell me about the others.

JAIMEY: There's only one other one. I mean I'd had flings here and there; some promising, and some infatuous. Honestly, they were stupid-I don't know what I was thinking. Love is blind, I guess.

MAREN: Aha! Caught you with a cliché! Sorry. Go on.

JAIMEY: 'You okay?

MAREN: I'm good. I just wanted to make a point.

JAIMEY: That sometimes it can't be helped?

MAREN: Yes and that they fit the meaning to a tee.

JAIMEY: Sometimes. That was a Freudian slip and I'm sorry I said it. And although I'll fight to the death for my own words, I'll have to agree on your point. But it's not enough for love. Not this.

MAREN: Fair enough. But would you agree that clichés are sometimes used by people who otherwise wouldn't be able to describe what they're feeling? It may not be the best description . . . it may even be frustratingly far from what they're feeling but they have to settle.

JAIMEY: I agree with that too. But that's why I hate them. Because they're not it. They're not enough to settle with. It was precisely this frustration that put me into action.

You know what? I lied. There were four-not three. My first was freedom.

MAREN: Okay, but in the beginning I told you I wanted none of that 'I love my mom and life' stuff. But I'm interested so go on.

JAIMEY: You won't regret this, I promise. See, my need for freedom brought me to London.

MAREN: Were you being held captive?

JAIMEY: Well I've already told you about the arranged marriage thing. On top of that, I was in many ways being held captive, yes. You'd be surprised at how many different facets there are to captivity besides actual physical imprisonment. And yes, the official second story encapsulated these facets but-

MAREN: —But you're not ready.

JAIMEY: . . . sorry.

MAREN: No, it's okay. Mind you, I have a suspicion that your love story lies within these unmentioned chapters. Like captivity, love has many facets. I'm sure that's a cliché but damn it, I'll use it.

JAIMEY: Ha! I see I've gotten into your head! But you may be right. But again, I'm not in a place where I can look back yet. I don't have a wide enough view for the proper description.

MAREN: I can see you're struggling and I understand completely. So let's put this in the back burner for now and move on to this third one. How'd you guys meet?

JAIMEY: We met in London . . .

MAREN: What's wrong?

JAIMEY: Maren, I changed my mind. I'm ready to talk about the second one. But not today. I have an appointment in an hour with another publisher about a book I'd been working on.

MAREN: What? Why didn't you ever tell me this? Congratulations! What's the book about?

JAIMEY: Thank you. It's a compilation of poetry that I'd written over the years. Like I said, I was pretty much held captive. I didn't have a voice. So I wrote instead.

MAREN: What's it called? When will it come out?

JAIMEY: Revelations for Genesis. It comes out in December.

MAREN: Well that's awesome. I can't wait to read it. Okay, I'll let you go but when will you be available for another chat?

JAIMEY: How about same time next week? Here.

MAREN: How about tomorrow?

JAIMEY: I have to prepare myself for this, Maren. I need time.

MAREN: The longer you wait, the more anxious you'll be. Believe me; I've been in many situations like this before.

JAIMEY: I don't know.

MAREN: Come on! Let's make it a dinner date. I'll buy you dinner and some drinks. That should calm the situation down. This coffee stuff wouldn't help at all.

In fact, I'll do you one better. I want to invite you to my home. That way, we won't have to worry about anyone hearing.

JAIMEY: Okay. Tomorrow at 6. Email me your address.

MAREN: Deal. I'll see you tomorrow.

Chapter 4

It was a case of choosing the lesser of two evils. This part of my past had been a sleeping giant up until now. The only time I'd ever talked about it was when it had actually occurred. Maren was right though. The sooner I went through this, the better. I'd already changed my mind a dozen times before I took the train to her house and I knew that had I waited until the following week, I would have called the whole thing off.

MAREN: Welcome to my home. I hope you like salmon. You're just in time; I have it all set up on the table. Do you like red or white?

JAIMEY: Salmon? White. And leave the carafe.

MAREN: Sure thing. Sounds like I'm in for quiet the story.

JAIMEY: I got raped.

MAREN: . . . . I . . . Wow. I don't know what to say.

JAIMEY: Sit. Let's do this.

MAREN: I'm sorry. Please. Go on.

JAIMEY: Well . . . I guess the right word for this one is, molested.

MAREN: I'm sorry; I thought we were going to talk about the third one.

JAIMEY: This is the third one.

MAREN: I'm sorry. Please go on.

JAIMEY: Stop apologizing. You don't need to. May I help myself to another glass?

MAREN: Please do.

JAIMEY: Nisha was my cousin. Her family had just relocated to California from India. Since they didn't have a place to stay, my parents took them in. Well, just her. My uncle lived right next door and since they had more space, they let her parents and her brother in.

At first, it was great having two playmates around. Since I was an only child and my parents would only let me leave the house to go to school, I didn't have much contact with other kids. But then, things changed. Since my uncle and aunt on my mom's side was living with us and had taken the spare room, my parents had us share my room.

This salmon is beautiful. Was it seared?

MAREN: Yes! Are you a foodie?

JAIMEY: MMM. Truly, Madly, Deeply.

MAREN: Really? Nice.

JAIMEY: Back in London, I used to experiment on the local produce and meats and used my flat mates as my own personal guinea pigs to see how the concoction turned out.

MAREN: I'm sure as students, they were really appreciative.

JAIMEY: At first, yes. But when they started to grow horizontally, everything turned to resentment.

MAREN: How funny!

JAIMEY: Yeah! Each time they'd realized how much weight they've gained, they'd look at me with murderous eyes. I couldn't help it though! I loved cooking. I loved seeing the satisfaction in people's faces after they've had their fill. And especially when their tongue touches that first morsel and they're immersed into this world of intense new flavors. I've often wished that I could stop time to savor those moments of discovery for them. I love showing people new things. I love teaching them about the world outside their own.

MAREN: That's very noble of you. I didn't realize how romantic food could be.

JAIMEY: Noble? Nah. It's just a way of reminding me of my own excitement when I'd finally decided to move out of my house. It was . . . well, it was down right, utopic.

MAREN: That's beautiful.

JAIMEY: It all started with a story she'd told me, one night. A few months had gone by since we first started sharing the room together and I'd become accustomed to her presence. I was comfortable with Nisha. We'd stay up way past our bed times to talk about absolutely everything. She'd patiently listen to all of my feelings about being lonely and trapped as an only child to two parents with very different backgrounds.

MAREN: How were they different?

JAIMEY: Dad's a conservative Hindu and was born and bred in New Delhi. Mom's a Roman Catholic Filipina. Until she met my dad, she was quite a progressive and radical feminist. I know this from all of the wild stories I'd overheard whenever her and her sister got together.

MAREN: Wow. It must have been confusing.

JAIMEY: My life was like a constant riddle back then. Mom, after getting married, had become very submissive. She'd given up a lot of her individuality and had given in to the role of the proverbial Indian housewife. Dad's family never accepted her though. He was born in the highest possible level of the caste system. It was the level closest to

God. People below him had to talk to him to talk to God. Marrying mom was not just a mere act of breaking familial laws, it was sacrilegious.

MAREN: Geez. Harsh.

JAIMEY: .... Maren. It's not my intention to interrupt the main story for small talk. I just need a little break once in a while.

MAREN: No, I understand. Take your time.

JAIMEY: There was a girl, Nisha said, who used to always wait for her at the front gates of her house each morning so they could walk together to school. She'd described her to me to a tee. This girl didn't go to her school. She went to the public high school that was a little further down the street. She'd always wear ripped jeans and t-shirts with band logos imprinted on them. For months and months, they'd have this walk to school together, during which they'd talk about anything and everything. Nisha's favorite subject was sex and relationships. I don't remember anything more but I remember her telling me about how the girl had kissed her one day, and how she'd panicked to the point that it marked the end of their friendship.

This was when it started.

MAREN: The abuse.

JAIMEY: She went on to talk about the kind of kiss it was. It wasn't the peck on the cheek like normal girls would give other girls to show affection. She'd kissed her passionately on the lips.

After some time of not seeing each other however, she said that she began to miss that girl. She'd realized, after sometime that this girl was extraordinarily beautiful. And that she was one of those people who didn't have to put effort into her looks.

Nisha'd missed all the attention that she'd gotten from her and upon reflecting about the day it had ended—that kiss. She kept referring to that kiss. She described it as if it was a character in itself. And then as if dissatisfied by the description, she asked me to be still so that she could show me how it was.

MAREN: Oh, dear.

JAIMEY: That marked the beginning of it all. I don't know why I didn't push her away. It was as if her demand for staying still had somehow disabled my ability to move. She whispered for me to sit up and held me against the wall. And pressing one shoulder down gently with her left hand . . . and slowly moving it up to my neck . . . and then cheek . . . . she raised her right one to my breast and stretched her neck out to kiss each of my lips-first the top, sucking it in between hers, then the bottom followed by a little peck . . . and then she pulled back and looked at me. She was searching my face for a reaction. When she found none, she slowly reached back in and pressed her lips against mine while slipping in her tongue.

MAREN: Whew.

JAIMEY: When it was over, she sat back with a conquering look on her face and said, "Like that."

I didn't say anything. Over the months that she'd been with me, I developed a lot of respect for her. She used to tell me stories of great adventures with her friends and family-ones that I'd always wished that I'd be able to do. I looked up to her. The way she would enjoy and take advantage of every little thing around her; the way she could manipulate monotony to something exciting and new-this intrigued me, for some reason.

My admiration for her had shut me down completely. And in the year or so that followed, she took full advantage of it.

MAREN: And you?

JAIMEY: Me?

MAREN: Did you ever talk to anyone about it?

JAIMEY: No. Not while it was happening. In the beginning, I was confused. I didn't know what was going on. I was so sheltered. My dad would tell me to close my eyes and cover my ears whenever the subject of sex came up on television or in real life. He'd even make me do that when characters showed affection in Disney Movies. The scenes when Aladdin kissed Jasmine put an embargo on Disney in the household for a long time.

MAREN: Wow. You didn't know.

JAIMEY: This type of thing, looking back now . . . I see it as quiet possibly the most diabolical form of violation.

MAREN: Go on.

JAIMEY: At least when you're raped, even if you can't move, you know in your consciousness that it's wrong and you hate the person who's doing it to you. With this . . . I-

MAREN: . . . You fell for her?

JAIMEY: Does this disgust you?

MAREN: No. You were a child. There were all kinds of bad things going on in your life. In its own demented way, this brought you much needed affection. It was false, but I imagine that you would have taken it in any form just the same.

JAIMEY: I was fat. My parents made me wear things that other kids used to tease me about. They themselves used to laugh at my appearance and make jokes about it when company was over.

This... what we had... made me not care. She made me feel... beautiful.

Listen, is this enough? I'd like to stop.

MAREN: Yes, but just one more thing. How did it end?

JAIMEY: My mom caught us in bed. Well, we were caught twice but the second time was what ended it.

MAREN: Who caught you the first time?

JAIMEY: Our aunt. This was a pretty fucked up situation now that I look back.

MAREN: Besides the obvious, how so?

JAIMEY: She'd somehow twisted the story around to make it look like it was my fault. And since I was the mutt-spawn of an outsider, my aunt sided with her.

MAREN: How did your aunt react when she first saw you guys?

JAIMEY: She'd walked into the room and as soon as she saw us, she walked immediately back out.

When she caught me alone that day, she lectured me on why that sort of thing was wrong.

MAREN: What did you say to her? Did she tell your parents?

JAIMEY: I couldn't say anything. She wouldn't have believed me.

Do you mind if I smoke?

MAREN: No. It's okay. I'll get you something for the ashes.

JAIMEY: Thanks. It's a habit I'd started in London. Everyone and their dogs smoke there.

MAREN: Yeah! I went there for a conference last month.

JAIMEY: Really?

MAREN: Yes. It was beautiful but it always bothered me that there was a pub in every other building. And you're right. They smoke as if the cigarette was an inhaler and they were hyperventilating.

JAIMEY: Yeah! London Fog, nothing. That shiznit's the smoke from all those fags.

MAREN: Ha!

JAIMEY: Serious. Now San Francisco bay-that's where you get the real fog. I used to walk outside in the morning feeling like I was literally in a cloud-like some ecological disaster from the stratosphere had occurred and the sky had suddenly fallen.

MAREN: Wow. Now that's something I'd love to see. I've never actually been to the west coast.

JAIMEY: You should go! Words will never do it justice.

MAREN: I plan to, actually. On my next vacation, California's definitely at the top of the list.

JAIMEY: Good!

MAREN: Listen Jaimey, we can do this another day if you like.

JAIMEY: No. We're almost done. I want this done.

MAREN: Okay. Whatever you say-you have the wheel here.

JAIMEY: She told my parents everything she'd seen and my cousin's version of the truth.

MAREN: What happened?

JAIMEY: Nothing. Thankfully, they hated their sister-in-law so they deemed every word that came out of her mouth as bullshit. All they did was ask me. I denied it. And that was the end of that.

But when my mom caught us, it was different.

MAREN: What did she do?

JAIMEY: At first, the same thing as my aunt—she immediately went back out and shut the door. As we were hurrying to put our clothes back on, I heard her walk into the room next door where my dad was watching TV. I'd only heard them murmuring but I could imagine every syllable that she might have said to him, and vice versa.

MAREN: How intense you must have felt. Did your cousin say anything?

JAIMEY: Nothing. We didn't speak. After she'd dressed, she left without saying anything to anyone. Later, when I'd finally summed up enough courage to go downstairs, my dad called me into the living room and told me to sit down on the chair that they'd set up next to the coffee table between him and mom.

"You lied to us," he said, "you looked at me, straight in the face and lied. You dirty girl, look at me."

My eyes had been affixed to a crumb at the foot of the table. In all the time that he was speaking, I'd been wondering as to the type of food it could have been. It was orange so I thought it was a Cheeto or a piece of the Filipino rice crackers that my mom had brought home from work the other night.

MAREN: It's amazing how you can remember this in such detail after all these years.

JAIMEY: Time stops at defining moments so that you can remember them exactly as how it happened.

I'd been raped three times besides this: Once as a child by a male cousin . . . Once, in an alley at school when they sent me to learn how to swim. A friend of the family suggested that it'd help me lose weight. The other time happened after the thing with Nisha-by dad's own hand-picked suitor. I can describe to you, in detail about the outfit of each person I came across and the weather to its exact degree in each of those days.

MAREN: My God. Did you ever tell your parents about them?

JAIMEY: No because the first time, it was family. His mom was taking care of me while my parents were working in another country. Plus a lot of other girls were involved and if I said anything, they'd be put on the spotlight. It didn't seem to bother them so I felt wrong to speak out. The second, I only told Nisha about.

MAREN: What did she say?

JAIMEY: She tried to comfort me and told my parents that she heard that the instructor was an ex-convict. She asked me not to tell them about what happened though. She said that it'd stain the family name and my dad would never forgive me.

I didn't tell anyone about the third because of how they reacted with Nisha. It would have made my parents' perception of me even worse than what it already was. And I couldn't go through that again.

MAREN: I'm so-

JAIMEY: —don't be. So in the living room, when I'd finally brought myself to raise my head to look at my dad in the face, he surprisingly turned away. For that instant, I felt-I don't know. It's weird but I felt as if I was understood. And that he'd turned his head because he couldn't bear to see the truth about what had happened. I was his daughter, in that moment. And I was bruised intentionally by someone in his own family.

I might have gotten off the hook easily now that I think about it. My dad had been so stressed from his job and his side of the family that every time I made a mistake, he'd hit me. My mistakes could range from using a pungent lotion that stunk up the entire car on a road trip to Reno to asking questions about the picture of Lord Shiva hanging behind the entrance of his room.

This time, he didn't hit me. All he told me was to go upstairs and not come down until he said so.

"What happened happened. We'll not speak of it again. Now go upstairs to your room and stay there until I tell your mama to call you. And close

the door. I don't even want to accidentally see your face."

After that, my cousin moved out. Dad himself packed up all of her stuff in my room and had personally taken it over next door.

A couple of months later, her family moved out to an apartment a few minutes, drive from the house. We'd see each other once in a while. But she'd never speak to me or even make eye contact.

MAREN: Did you want her to?

JAIMEY: Yes. She made me believe that I loved her. Like I said, I was beautiful in her eyes. I couldn't handle them not seeing me in that way again.

MAREN: I hope it's clear to you now that you were an undeniable victim of abuse.

JAIMEY: Me too.

MAREN: Jaimey, it's true. You didn't know.

JAIMEY: There was this one time I caught her alone in a room of her apartment for a few minutes. I was desperate. I had to ask.

MAREN: What?

JAIMEY: If she still loved me. If she could forgive me for everything that happened after mom caught us in the act.

She couldn't even look at me. She put her hand on the door knob and before exiting, looked down at the floor and whispered, "No. I don't love you."

I tried to comfort myself by thinking that she'd said it for my sake-so as to help me move on. I just . . .

MAREN: You just?

JAIMEY: I hated that she didn't look at me. If I saw her eyes, I would have known the truth. I guess I should have been glad that I didn't. I guess. I don't know.

MAREN: Where is she now?

JAIMEY: Back in Cali-married and successful with kids. Over the years, my feeling for her had faded and given rise to the truth. If I think about it too much, I still sometimes find myself confused.

MAREN: About what?

JAIMEY: About how love can be so deceptive, or how the world can have the audacity to use love as a tool for deception.

Anyway, there's your story. It's getting late, I should be off.

MAREN: Thank you for this. It couldn't have been easy.

JAIMEY: You're welcome. It's . . . It was necessary.

MAREN: Yes.

JAIMEY: You're wrong you know. I'm not a victim. I'm alive. I'm breathing and I'm doing okay. That's not a definition for a victim.

MAREN: You're a survivor.

JAIMEY: Not even that. I didn't survive. I lived. And I live.

Email me to set up the next appointment Maren. Thanks for having me. Goodnight.

MAREN: Goodnight, Jaimey.

Chapter 5

Maren emailed me the next day to set another appointment for the following week. As soon as I'd received her message, I booked a plane ticket to Spain. I needed to get away.

There'd been some unfinished business left for me to take care of in Barcelona. When a friend of mine invited me to meet him there, I took it as a sign telling me that it was time to finally get this chapter of my life closed.

December passed by, and a week after a month's worth of continuous travelling to and through California and Spain, Maren had finally caught me back home. I was too exhausted to put up a fight. I did, however muster up enough strength to prolong it.

MAREN: Welcome back! It's so good to see you. It's been over a month!

JAIMEY: Thank you, yes. It's been a while. After I left for Spain, I felt the urge to keep travelling.

MAREN: Where else did you go?

JAIMEY: I went to Charlotte to visit a friend, and then high-tailed it to California for Christmas with the parents. I didn't even unpack when I got back home because the next day, I flew to Chicago to meet with friends for a road trip to Las Vegas to celebrate the New Years.

MAREN: Wow! What an adventure! You cleared like . . . 70% of the globe!

JAIMEY: Yeah! I wish I could keep going. I wish I could make the world, my home. My kitchen would be in the beaches of Barceloneta and the living room would be in Paris. I'd make my office in London and the front yard, California.

MAREN: Where would New York be?

JAIMEY: My bedroom. Rome and India would be the spare bedrooms and the Philippines would be the back yard where the pool area would also be.

MAREN: What a home that would make. I hope you achieve that someday.

JAIMEY: Thank you. I'm so close; I could almost smell the fresh cuttlefish on the grill.

MAREN: Speaking of, what did you do in Barcelona? You told me that you had some special business to take care of, and that you also met with a friend.

JAIMEY: This could be another story in itself.

MAREN: Oh? Go on.

JAIMEY: My parents met in Barcelona. My dad snuck into the country in a train from France. They had me there.

MAREN: But your application said that you were born in the Philippines.

JAIMEY: It also said that I was born in October.

MAREN: You mean you lied?

JAIMEY: That's what I went to Barcelona for. To see if I'd inadvertently lied.

My friend had originally planned to come visit me here. But I needed to get away from the states. I'd just found out that I had family living here and getting in touch with them had always lead to some sort of drama. I wanted to steer clear of that. And I have to be honest with you-our last session took a lot out of me.

MAREN: I could see that. I don't blame you.

JAIMEY: Thank you for understanding. I think I should tell you a little something about my relationship with Chris.

MAREN: Is it juicy?

JAIMEY: Well, we're talking about love. It fits, but it comes from another person's perspective.

I met Chris in London during the second term. He was a study abroad student from a University in Michigan. Chris is twice my height and has the football player build.

MAREN: Ooh, I like it already.

JAIMEY: Ha! Yeah. Anyway, my flat mates and I had appointed ourselves the friendly neighborhood welcoming committee and when we found out that there was a newbie moving in, we took it upon ourselves to well, welcome him.

When we'd first seen him, being the rowdy and playful college chicks that we were, Hannah and I had both agreed that he was very attractive and it was decided that we'd play with him for a little bit.

At that point, I'd only gone as far as flirting with the guys I'd met. I didn't want to be in a relationship. I was too focused in my determination to get a work visa and to land a job as a writer. But this didn't mean that I couldn't have a little fun. I'd only known freedom for three months since I'd moved to London. And I wanted to experience every grain of what it had to offer. So in the spirit of the excitement, I played along.

Hannah was involved with a guy in Birmingham whom she'd met in a cruise back in the west coast but at the time, Dick still hadn't asked her to be his official girlfriend so to her, whatever she did would have still been within her rights.

Something happened that night and Hannah left the scene for a little while so I did what I would normally do when the flat has visitors and decided to cook for him.

Back home, I'd be shy whenever I'd meet a stranger and all conversations would revolve around work and other redundant boring stuff. I promised myself, before getting on the plane that this monotony was going to change. And sure enough, each time I met anyone after that, I'd speak to them as if they were long-time friends.

Chris was taken aback by this. There was not one hour that had passed without him having to shake his head in laughter and tell me how different I was from any other girl he'd met before.

As time passed, my demeanor had slowly made him comfortable enough to reveal to me about the family he'd come from. Much like me he'd also gone through neglect and abuse from his father.

At first, he was reluctant to open up. But in telling him bits and pieces of my own past, the similarities had brought us closer.

The guy was basically depressed. He felt that in moving to London, he'd abandoned his obligations as a son and brother to his family. On top of that, he was in a financial nightmare. Chris would go days without having anything to eat.

MAREN: So it was a perfect match! You loved to cook, and he needed to eat.

JAIMEY: No. It was no match. I was in a far different place than him. And as for the food bit, I wish it would have been that easy.

MAREN: It wasn't?

JAIMEY: Not at all. The guy was a man's man. He was too proud to ask for any help. He was used to carrying the world on his own shoulders. He would have never have asked me to share the load.

The best and only thing that I could do for Chris was to listen. And I understood him. Over time, he'd developed a reputation as an obsessed weirdo.

Wait. I'm getting ahead of myself. I need to tell you about that one night first.

MAREN: What one night?

JAIMEY: I'll get there. Don't worry. But even before that, you have to know the kind of person I am when it comes to the attraction game.

MAREN: Okay. What kind of person are you?

JAIMEY: Oblivious. I wouldn't know if you were attracted to me unless you blatantly said it. And even then, you'd have to say it in a serious tone. Otherwise, I'd simply shrug it off as banter.

MAREN: Did Chris like you?

JAIMEY: Yes. And he came on to me in the most obvious way possible, that one night.

MAREN: Oh? How?

JAIMEY: Well the flat mates were hanging out in my room and we had all been drinking. Chris was living upstairs in another flat but I'd invited him to come and meet my friends. The night was like any other night of get-togethers. We were all chatting and goofing around but Chris, in his usual introverted ways, would only speak when spoken to. I would try to include him in all of the conversations and to joke with him to get him comfortable with the crowd. Chris felt awkward in a room full of people but he did pretty well that night.

When everyone had finally left, we were still talking. Of what? I don't know. But all of a sudden, he stood up and bent over the bed where I'd been sitting.

MAREN: And?

JAIMEY: And he planted one on me.

He picked an awesome moment too. Genuwine's Pony was playing on the radio. I was only human. The alcohol and the sexual tone of the music had put me in the mood to reciprocate.

It was intense. When he saw that I was into it, he picked me up as I wrapped my legs around his waist, swung me around and pinned me against the wall.

MAREN: Whoa! Is getting hot in here? Or is it just me?

JAIMEY: I know what you mean. But we didn't do anything that night. As was always the case, I managed to get him out of the room to stop the situation from going any further than just playing around. I liked Chris. But in that moment, this great awareness came over me that told me that I needed to stop. The way he was kissing me was not a mere act of in fatuous attraction. I needed it to stop.

In the days that followed, he'd tried to get in touch with me. Calling me every other hour each day and knocking at the flat door each afternoon.

And then it turned a little weird.

MAREN: Weird?

JAIMEY: Yes. Chris was drinking a lot. He could down an entire bottle of Hennessey in one sitting, which I think he did and often.

It got to the point where he'd knock on my door at 3am, so loud that it would shake the walls of my room.

MAREN: That's scary.

JAIMEY: Yes. At the time, I was really concerned. I knew that he wouldn't go as far as hurting me or anything. Chris never meant any harm. I just couldn't handle him and me at the same time. So I tried the best I could to ignore him. There was a door that separated my flat from all of the other flats so he'd have to knock at that door before he could get to mine. I'd asked all of my flat mates to tell him that I wasn't home or too busy to speak to him if ever he'd come knocking or looking for me.

I gotta say this again-he wasn't a bad guy. He just needed a friend who he could talk to. And to some degree, I was also to blame for his outbursts. Had I even once stopped and listened to him, I bet it would have calmed everything down.

From that time on, my flat mates had begun to see him as weird and demented. I completely blame myself for that. Chris had given me a chance to see where he'd come from. He'd given me a personal tour of his soul. This is no easy task, especially coming from such a proud man as he was.

MAREN: No, I bet it wasn't.

JAIMEY: But things got better. Over time, he'd learned to be calmer and apologized to me for his actions. Of course, I'd forgiven him. To a certain extent, I felt like he didn't need to apologize. It was my duty to be there for him. In fact, I was the one who needed to apologize. I don't know that I ever did.

Towards the end of the term, Chris asked me to be his girlfriend but I knew I couldn't. I'd grown quiet fond of Chris but it was never to the point where I wanted to be in a committed relationship with him.

MAREN: How did you break it to him?

JAIMEY: I've always been the kind of person who'd avoid saying, no to people. I knew that this was his final term so I put it to him, gently. I told him that I wasn't in the position to be in a relationship at the moment. But that if he was to remain in London, it'd be a different story. I said that I'd been in a long-distance relationship before and that it had ended badly. I couldn't bring myself to ever do that again.

MAREN: How did he react to that?

JAIMEY: He came back.

MAREN: What?!

JAIMEY: Yep.

MAREN: Man. Even with all of his obligations back home?

JAIMEY: He hates home. That part was easy. I know that London was where he'd wanted to be and he told me on the night that he'd returned that there were many other reasons why he'd made the move.

But then, he reminded me of our talk about how I said I'd consider being with him if he'd stayed in London and that was mostly why he'd wanted to return so badly.

MAREN: How did you feel about that?

JAIMEY: Guilty as fuck! A lot of things had happened while he was away. That summer in fact, was when I met . . .

MAREN: When you met . . . ?

JAIMEY: Her.

MAREN: Okay, the way you just said that brought chills down my spine. Is this the fourth one?

JAIMEY: Fourth and final, yes.

MAREN: I see. Please. Continue.

JAIMEY: On top of everything else, I'd given up on trying to stay there. I'd decided, over that summer that I'd move here.

MAREN: And did you tell him about what was going on?

JAIMEY: By that time, the girl had moved to Paris. She was on a ten week stay but London consisted only of half of the program.

But I did tell him about her. We weren't together or anything but I . . .

I don't know. You see, I may come off as the eccentric hippie-the people loving, anti-commitment making, lover of the world, but when I fall for someone, that's it. I couldn't get over her. And I was honest with him.

MAREN: How did he react?

JAIMEY: He didn't take it seriously. There was something about lesbian relationships that made it not serious to him.

MAREN: Did that make you angry?

JAIMEY: Yes. I'm a die-hard feminist. But I somehow managed to ignore that feeling to prepare myself in telling him my other news.

MAREN: New York

JAIMEY: Yes.

MAREN: How did he take it?

JAIMEY: I think you can imagine how he must have taken it. But Chris is a sensitive guy. After giving him some time to take in what I'd just told him, he said to me that all he wanted for me was to be happy.

MAREN: Did this happen on that same night?

JAIMEY: Yes.

MAREN: Wow. That was quick.

JAIMEY: Well he did struggle with it, a bit. I remember one night, he told me that all I had to do was to say the word and that he'd move to NY with me.

MAREN: Really!? Geez. The guy had it bad for you.

JAIMEY: I don't know. I still think that at that point in his life, he'd only come across a few truly good people. I wholeheartedly cared about him. And he knew this because of the fact that I didn't completely shun him after what had happened during his breakdown in the previous term. And a lot of people were using him. He knew that I'd never even consider doing that.

I believe that he thought he'd loved me. But had he opened up to the right people, I know that he'd see that given the chance, they'd also handle his situation in the same way.

The week before I moved here, he made me promise that if in a couple of years, if I was still single, I'd give him a chance at a real relationship with me.

MAREN: Was it a sincere promise?

JAIMEY: Yes, for two reasons. One, being with Chris makes me feels safe. All my life, I'd always counted only on myself to deal with things. I always had my eyes open for any and all dangers that might pop up. Chris helped me to realize how tiring it is to carry all of that baggage on my own. He'd somehow managed to convince me that I could trust him with some of the load. With Chris, I felt protected.

MAREN: But you didn't love him.

JAIMEY: Not in the way that he wanted.

Wouldn't it be great to be able to manipulate your feelings?

MAREN: Why do you ask?

JAIMEY: I wish I loved him. He was a great guy. On top of everything that I told you, I believe that he would make the perfect husband and father. Had I loved him, the world would have leaned a little bit more to my side.

MAREN: So you felt that even in living away from your family and away from the past, that the world was still out to get you?

JAIMEY: The past is the past but memories will always be present. It's like an incurable disease, the past. Given time, you learn to live with it, but you're never going to get rid of it.

MAREN: Have you ever tried therapy?

JAIMEY: Have I ever! My primary care doctor had suggested therapy for me a few years ago. I was hospitalized a lot for dehydration and kidney trouble. She believed that this was self-induced.

MAREN: Was it?

JAIMEY: I wouldn't eat. At first, it was unintentional. But later on, I'd discovered that it was the only way that I had control of anything. And doctors-you can't lie to doctors. One checkup and blood test and they pretty much know your entire life history.

MAREN: Did you go?

JAIMEY: For a while, but it didn't work. They put me on medication that had me in the fetal position on my bed for most days. And I wasn't able to open up to them. I didn't know them. They were being paid by the money of the people who'd put me in that state. How could I say anything?

Plus, they didn't need to find a cure for me. I'd already known. Freedom was my cure and writing, my prescription.

You know, a day before my flight to London I went to the hospital for a final blood test. The doctors had me go every week for it so as to make sure my organs were working properly.

MAREN: Were they alright when you went?

JAIMEY: No. In fact, my kidneys had gotten so bad that the doctor wanted to admit me to the hospital.

MAREN: So you had to postpone your trip.

JAIMEY: No. I postponed my death. I had to go.

I told the doc about my situation and how I had to fly out the following day, but she wouldn't listen. She told me that if I didn't follow her advice, if I didn't go into dialysis, that I wouldn't live to see the next year.

MAREN: What did you do?

JAIMEY: I asked her for a few hours to get my business affairs in order and to let my parents and boss know what was going on. And she let me go. And I left. And I never went back.

MAREN: I'm speechless.

JAIMEY: I had to. If I'd stayed, I knew that it'd mean an even sooner death than anything that could ever appear on her prognosis. I simply had to go.

MAREN: Are you okay now? It's been a year, right?

JAIMEY: Yes. I'm alright. And yes, it's been a year! That's why I wanted to celebrate it by honoring the very thing that had saved my life.

MAREN: Ah! Travel.

JAIMEY: Yes. The world, the people whom I'd shared it with, and the freedom that came of all of it. On the first of this month, I'd rung in the New Year with my friends from the top of the world. We went skydiving! I was alive! And it was . . . beautiful.

MAREN: What a story.

JAIMEY: Yes, I've been blessed with many of them. To hell with death-with my words, I am immortalized.

So anyway, back to the story. Chris had originally planned on coming here for a visit but I suggested to him that we should meet in Spain. I know that he'd always wanted to visit there and he'd been trying to learn Spanish since Kingdom come. He agreed. I didn't tell him about my mission.

MAREN: Yes, about that. What was it exactly?

JAIMEY: I wanted to hunt down my birth certificate. I wanted to know that the romantic notions about my being born there were not lies. And . . .

MAREN: Yes?

JAIMEY: Dad-whenever he'd get angry, he'd express regret of having me. I wouldn't admit it for a while but I wanted to see his name written on that paper. I don't fully understand why I needed this. Maybe it was because I had doubts that I was even his. Before I'd become a citizen, my passport had me with my mom's last name. Whenever a customs rep would ask for an explanation, he would say that I was my mom's daughter. Not his.

Growing up, it didn't really bother me. This is why I'm not really sure as to where this need to know came from. Back in Cali, I don't think I ever doubted that I was his. At times though, I wished I wasn't. And on those times when he had to explain himself to customs, I felt a certain pleasure when I he would say those words.

Anyway, my plan was to go to the hospital where they'd once told me that I was born. I'd figured that someone there would be able to direct me to the right path.

MAREN: You told your parents about this, then?

JAIMEY: No. I had to be sly about it and ask passively whenever mom would call.

MAREN: How did Chris feel about this?

JAIMEY: He was awesome. He'd become really ill during the entire trip but even with that, he supported me and was there for me every step of the way.

The street where I was born seemed to be coiled from end to end of Barcelona's borders. We'd been walking in search for that God forsaken hospital for what had seemed to be days to me. I can't imagine, especially with his flu what Chris had been going through.

MAREN: So you guys didn't find it?

JAIMEY: No. A security guard of some random building we'd walked into said that the hospital was no longer there. El Corte Ingles, the famous mall had expanded to and through the area and where the hospital stood had become a Coach shop.

MAREN: What did you do?

JAIMEY: Chris wasn't convinced. I'd been speaking Spanish with the people I'd met so I had to translate to him. But after the guard, I'd become so discouraged that I didn't want to talk about it. At that point, I was ready to give up. His he-man, save-the-lady-in-distress was awakened when Chris saw this. He wanted to keep searching.

That night, we were supposed to move to another hotel so I finally managed to convince him that it was time to call it a night.

MAREN: Why'd you have to move hotels?

JAIMEY: We overbooked. We each reserved hotels thinking that each other had not. The first hotel that we went to was the one that he booked. This one was mine, so we decided to check it out.

MAREN: I see.

JAIMEY: After registering with the concierge, Chris told me to go on ahead to the room because he needed to ask the front desk about something. He wouldn't tell me what but I had the feeling that he was still on it about the hospital.

I didn't want to deal with it anymore so I went to the room.

About an hour later, he came upstairs with the biggest grin on his face.

MAREN: He found the hospital?

JAIMEY: No. The hospital was gone but this was better. He found a way to get my certificate.

He told me that the concierge had someone on the phone waiting for me to give me information on exactly how to get the paper.

MAREN: Wow! What a guy!

JAIMEY: Exactly! But I'm not done. The hotel I'd found was destiny. It was as if God himself had made the reservation.

MAREN: Huh?

JAIMEY: Before getting on the phone, the concierge told me that Chris had asked him about how people could get their birth records. A few years back, the government had gotten rid of all the birth documents dating before 1990 but they'd recorded the data into an electronic referencing system. He said that if I wanted to retrieve my old documents, all I had to do was go to the Civil Registrar's department.

MAREN: That sounds easy enough.

JAIMEY: You have no idea, Maren. It turned out that the Hotel was right in front of the building!

MAREN: No way!

JAIMEY: Yes! I couldn't believe my luck. It couldn't have been luck. This was too close to miraculous for that. No, it was destiny.

MAREN: So the guy on the phone . . . .

JAIMEY: The guy on the phone was a friend of the concierge who'd also gone through the process of trying to find his documents. The problem now was that he'd told me that I needed the page and section number of the original certificate in order to find it, as well as valid identification. I had neither.

MAREN: You couldn't use your passport?

JAIMEY: No. I was born with a different name and my mom had long since lost the papers so I didn't have the information. I might as well have been back to square one.

I tried to explain this to Chris but the jerk wouldn't budge. His persistence was getting annoying. At that point, all I wanted to do was drink and enjoy whatever time we had left in the city.

MAREN: What did you guys end up doing?

JAIMEY: I decided to humor him and went to the office anyway.

MAREN: What a guy. He was determined.

JAIMEY: That's Chris. But that night and the days after, he'd become different.

MAREN: How?

JAIMEY: Finding out that we'd ended up right in front of the building had literally changed his entire outlook in his beliefs. You see, Chris is agnostic. He didn't believe in God or fate or any of that spiritual stuff. Whatever success he'd gained since birth, he believed that it was from his own doing. And whatever his goals were in life, he felt that no one but himself would be responsible in attaining.

He couldn't get over it. He'd kept repeating, and chuckling and shaking his head, much like how he acted back when he'd first met me, that this was something more than coincidence and that he might have to re-evaluate his entire belief system after this. Even he said that this was something more than mere luck. Chris was positively amazed.

MAREN: Me and him both.

JAIMEY: There's more.

MAREN: What?

JAIMEY: I didn't find out for sure until after I'd returned from the trip but there was a Church right behind the government building that had caught my mind with a murderous grip. I'd experience a haunting moment each time we'd pass it. The surrounding paths were filled with people but the courtyard and the church always remained empty.

The buildings were tall and except for some strips of light from crevices in between each one of them, the block was dark and full of shadows of the statues spread around. That area of the church however, seemed unreasonably darker.

I spoke to my mom when I got home and asked her about the churches where they'd gotten married and where I was baptized. And you might not believe this but she said that they did them both in the same church that was less than a two minute walking distance from the Government building where they'd registered their marriage.

MAREN: Again, speechless. No . . . freakin..way.

JAIMEY: Yes, freakin way.

MAREN: I don't know what to say. Your life is a romance novel.

JAIMEY: Isn't it? I still can't believe it.

But back to my story-Chris was pumped. He wanted to know that we'd exhausted all possible options in getting that certificate before we went back home. And I'd given up in trying to persuade him that I'd gotten over it.

MAREN: Were you over it?

JAIMEY: No. It killed me. But I didn't want to hear another discouraging news. I wouldn't have known how to handle it.

MAREN: But you went anyway. For him.

JAIMEY: I guess. No. It was for me too. I knew he was right. I'd regret not having gone. And I'm so thankful that I did.

MAREN: What happened?

JAIMEY: We were passed around between different departments within the building. We were both starving because we hadn't eaten all day and the past night. But finally, we were lead to a section of the office full of people waiting for their numbers to be called up.

I'd gotten fed up with waiting so I went straight to the open window. The man behind the counter was flirtatious and kept asking me things about myself. I thought that it was no wonder that it was taking so much time for them to help each person. But I kept my cool and decided to use the situation to my advantage.

I'd brought my passport with me but I didn't want to take it out until I absolutely had to.

MAREN: Did you have to?

JAIMEY: No! It was crazy!

I told the man that I was there to see if he could help me find my certificate without knowing the filing number.

"Pues, para ti, si." He said. *For you, yes.*

He asked me for the first and last name. Now, mind you Maren I was not lying. He'd asked me for 'the' name and not 'my' name.

MAREN: Ha-ha, what did you say?

JAIMEY: I said Sonia Corpuz.

MAREN: Your real name.

JAIMEY: Yes. And when he asked for 'the birthday,' I said December 12.

MAREN: Did he do it?

JAIMEY: And wished me a happy birthday!

MAREN: It was your birthday that you did this . . . your real birthday?

JAIMEY: Yes.

MAREN: What a romance.

JAIMEY: And he didn't even ask for an ID.

I can't. I don't have the words to tell you how I was feeling. It's impossible. He stamped a printed copy on official papers, a seal of certification of my birth certificate and handed it to me as if it were a brochure that he was passing out to everyone. I was . . . I was . . . . no. I can't explain it.

MAREN: Go Chris!

JAIMEY: Yes, indeed. In all my life, no one had ever supported me like this before. Chris is my hero. He'll never be able to understand the extent to it.

MAREN: I bet you also had quite an effect on him; not just as a person, but from the experience of it all.

JAIMEY: I'd never seen him so himself before. He was a very reserved guy-very quiet. But during those final days in Barcelona, he'd really let lose. He'd laugh, smile, and speak in one continuous, ecstatic tone. Indoors or not, he'd always have an outside voice. Chris was nothing but a blessing. I hope that during our lifetime, he'll come to know how much he's done for me. And even more so, I hope that when he finds a woman to love in the way that I felt that he'd loved me-the feeling will be reciprocated in at least the same extent. Chris not only needs it, he deserves it.

MAREN: I know that I'd asked you this on our first day through Skype but I can't help but ask again. You have a pattern in the way you speak about the people in your relationships and it's one of affection. In looking back now, in what you know of love Jaimey, and in the definition from all of these events that had happened from your life after sharing them with me, relationship wise, have you ever loved someone?

JAIMEY: From the stories that I'd told you thus far, I know now that the answer is no. But I shouldn't have deemed them as cliché. Affection is tailored to each relationship. Everyone should be free to call it as they see it fit.

Love, though; she belongs in a certain facet of spirituality. When I looked into my past partners' eyes, I saw a reflection of the room and I saw a blurry silhouette of myself. I'll deny this every time and I'll shoot you if you tell anyone but I'm the poster child of a hopeless romantic. In love, when I look into someone's eyes, I want to see God.

MAREN: In two years, given the opportunity, will you be open enough to see Him in Chris' eyes, I wonder.

JAIMEY: Me too; but, like I said, when I fall for someone. That's it.

MAREN: Wait. But you said you haven't yet.

JAIMEY: I said from the stories that I'd told you, I haven't.

MAREN: So you've seen God.

JAIMEY: I believe I might have.

MAREN: Please. Explain.

JAIMEY: I saw truth. And instead of a blurry silhouette of myself, I saw me.

MAREN: This was your fourth.

JAIMEY: And final.

MAREN: Final? Are you single?

JAIMEY: Yes. But spiritually, I'm taken.

MAREN: By God?

JAIMEY: By love.

Chapter 6

It was late when we'd left the coffee shop. The barista had to personally come over to our table to tell us that the store had been closed for an hour and that the staff was ready to go. I was more than happy to leave. I have managed, once again to avoid this last part of the story. But Maren was determined and had adamantly insisted on seeing me the following morning. This would be the last chapter so I forced myself to say yes to her in the hopes that I'd feel better when this was finally over with.

JAIMEY: You know how in the bible, God is never directly described?

MAREN: How do you mean?

JAIMEY: His power and presence is only ever described in parables.

MAREN: Were you planning on telling me a short story to describe your relationship with this person?

JAIMEY: No. Otherwise, I'd stop now. What I told you would be enough.

MAREN: Hmm. Go on.

JAIMEY: I don't know if the disciples felt that they were unworthy to talk about Him directly, but I'd always taken it as the reason. This whole thing that we have-it took so long to finish, because I used almost every chapter as an excuse to avoid this last one.

MAREN: I knew you were trying to. But the story about your cousin had taken me aback. In my opinion, most people would much rather talk about past heartbreaks than past traumatic events—especially ones as serious as what had happened to you.

JAIMEY: These were two different ball games. The other one was based on deception and illusions. This one was based on truth and realism.

Plus, it's been so long with that whole cousin thing.

Let me ask you something. Do you like to go to museums?

MAREN: Yes. We've got a lot of great ones in New York.

JAIMEY: When you look at a portrait, you don't look at it from an inch away do you?

MAREN: No, or I wouldn't be able to see the whole thing.

JAIMEY: Exactly. This is why I'd been reluctant to tell you this story. Where I am now is not far enough away for me to be able to give you the entire account.

MAREN: Fair enough. Having noted that, how about telling me what you see, then?

JAIMEY: I suppose I can do that.

MAREN: You sound disappointed.

JAIMEY: I've gotten accustomed to emptying my soul to you during our sessions. I don't want to break the streak, 'is all.

MAREN: I see what you're saying.

JAIMEY: I hope so. In the other stories, I was able to give you at least a glimpse of the kind of people involved. Even while travelling, I'd much rather bring my friends along than to tell them about the places that I've visited.

MAREN: Sounds expensive.

JAIMEY: The cost of not being able to experience the grandeur is far more expensive. I love them too much and I love travel too much for them not to make each other's acquaintance.

MAREN: You loved her.

JAIMEY: I just want to do her justice. I don't think any set of words exist that's descriptive enough to tell you who she was to me. If I could buy you a ticket to the past, I would.

MAREN: Ha-ha. What a trip, that would be.

Let's take this one at a time, shall we? How did you guys meet?

JAIMEY: It was at the start of the summer sessions. I'd just accepted a writing job with a web marketing company to keep myself busy during the 10-week break.

The flat was nearly empty from people who'd gone back home to visit their families. Those who were only there for one or two terms had moved out a week ago.

The emptiness and silence was driving me up the wall so when the new people moved in, I was only too glad.

MAREN: Was she one of them?

JAIMEY: Yes, Jade was one of them.

She came into the flat with Elaine, my new next door neighbor. The ruckus outside sparked my curiosity because the place had been empty the entire day. That's when I first met her.

They were both from the same state. Funnily enough, Chris is also from there.

MAREN: Really? Wow, the coincidences in the life you lead. It's positively amazing.

JAIMEY: I still can't believe it.

MAREN: Was it love at first sight?

JAIMEY: No. I didn't allow myself to consider the possibility of that ever happening with a woman. But I did think she was gorgeous. She had on a black and white striped top and a long black skirt that draped over her ankles. And it wasn't really a skirt. It was a sleeveless dress but she made it into one.

MAREN: What?

JAIMEY: What?

MAREN: You're smiling. What?

JAIMEY: No, I was just thinking about her versatility. That dress went a long way that summer. I remember one night when we went to a club. She took that dress and using only a few pins, made it into a pair of harem pants. Another time, she twisted it around her waist and somehow made it into a top that looked like it belonged in a store front display case of some high profile fashion shop that can only be found on the High Street.

MAREN: Wow. Now that is called versatility.

JAIMEY: Yeah. Her eye for fashion was really something. She redefined it, really. She could take something humble and simple and seemingly complete in its course in life like that dress and turn it into something more magnificent than what it was intended to become. I tell you, watching her work was inspired. Even her movements in front of that mirror . . . reaching to get another pin, bending over to clip together residual fragments of the cloth-it was like ballet; it was . . . all of it was art in action.

MAREN: Is that what attracted you to her?

JAIMEY: More than anything; it was this passion.

But I didn't see it as attraction in that way, at first. Up until that summer, I wasn't fully out of the closet about my sexuality.

MAREN: But, you were somewhat out?

JAIMEY: If I was asked about it, I'd say that I liked both or that I was indifferent when it came to gender. However, I'd always maintained the demeanor and mannerisms of a straight, female eccentric. And I lived it. I mean, when a gorgeous looking girl crossed paths with me, I would notice her but that was as far as it went until she came along.

MAREN: Yes, tell me more about that.

JAIMEY: Her gay-dar was uncanny. I remember asking her about her first impressions of me; she told me that she'd immediately figured it out from the moment I stepped out of my room to introduce myself.

Anyway, it was her first day in London and together with Elaine, whom she'd met on the plane ride over, went to explore the city before settling in to their new flats. I was surprised when Elaine told me that out of the entire list of places that they'd visited, she didn't see the famous Camden Market which was literally a 10 minute walk away from where we lived. And being the self-appointed ambassador of the city, I took it upon myself to invite them for a tour.

By the time we got there, all of the booths were closing so I took them for drinks in a Cuban restaurant hidden between the lock and the food booths.

I don't remember much about what we talked about but I know that she and I had agreed on everything that was brought up. I'd long since gotten used to speaking with strangers as if they were longtime friends but I kind of got the feeling that she was a bit shy. It was acceptable though. She'd just moved to another country for ten weeks, away from the normal family setting that she'd been used to all her life. But each time that we shared an idea or opinion, the excitement that I sensed behind her voice kept drawing my attention to her.

Now mind you, at this point I didn't detect these feelings as ones of attraction. The acknowledgement of my own sexuality had never been important enough for me to put any attention to it. I just went with the flow of things.

After our drinks we went to another bar where she bought us each our second or third tequila shots. We danced a little bit and after a while, decided to take the party back to my place where I made more drinks.

MAREN: Ah! College life; how I miss it.

JAIMEY: Me too! Not just for the drinking. I was working on my MBA but it was my first time really experiencing this college life. It was my first time for a lot of things. I was a living, breathing, ball of enthusiasm and I felt it to be my duty to share it with everyone.

MAREN: That's why you were the self-appointed tour guide.

JAIMEY: Yes. And on a deeper level, I just felt so blessed with this experience. I continue to struggle with religion but it was my faith that brought me to this.

My plate was overflowing with this . . . this knowledge of the key to true happiness. My eccentricities and weirdness came from this and in order for people to understand me, I needed for them to understand what I was feeling. That's why instead of talking about Camden Town, I brought them there. Likewise, it was for that same reason that instead of talking about the places I go, I bring my friends there.

I have the utmost respect for words but some things in life, you just have to experience-it's a phenomenon that once you feel, you're positively reborn.

Writing was my way. Elaine sketched. Jade did all that and was musically talented. And both of them were into fashion. In order to understand me, I needed London to grab their creative outlets from within their souls and pull them inside out.

MAREN: Did it work?

JAIMEY: I think it did. But no matter what the outcome, I had a great time doing it. Today, I am the self-appointed ambassador of the world. I'm always travelling in a never ending mission to show everyone-anyone who's willing to learn, what I'd learned and what I continue to learn. It's exciting! It's simply beautiful.

By the time Jade and I met, my soul had taken a 180 degree turn for the better things in life. I think this is precisely what had attracted her to me in the first place.

MAREN: And I think I've found a travel buddy.

JAIMEY: Yeah! You tell me where you want to go and when, and regardless of whether or not I've been there, I'll come with you and appoint myself, your honorary tour guide.

MAREN: It's a deal! But let's go back to your story—back to Jade. What happened?

JAIMEY: We had the time of our lives is what happened. We went back to my room where I invited them to taste my famous mojitos.

MAREN: What made it famous?

JAIMEY: The people who tasted it and woke up without having remembered ever going to sleep.

MAREN: Whoa! That sounds dangerous but fun at the same time.

Oh yeah, you told me, you had a thing for the kitchen.

JAIMEY: Yes. If I told you the ingredients, I'd have to kill you.

MAREN: Ha! Duly noted

JAIMEY: So we gathered in my room for a chat and listened to some music on my iTunes Library. When Adele came on, Jade asked us if we've ever heard, 'Rumor

Has It,' which was more upbeat than the other slow and depressing tunes we were used to hearing her sing. I'd never heard of that song and neither did Elaine. And at that, as if she was sitting on a spring, Jade jumped up, ran towards the computer and played it with the speakers on full blast.

If I could only connect my memory to a projector and show you her exact movements, I would because I tell you, time stood still for me.

It was like she was possessed by some spirit of dance. Each step and each wayward movement of her arms were marching to the rhythm of that music. It was no longer a simple number that DJ's would mix on the record. This was a tribal act; and she was worshipping the God responsible for creating it. After that, Elaine and I joined her and started dancing along. But only after that song, did I join in.

MAREN: Why?

JAIMEY: Her movements made it like she had a special bond with the beats. I didn't want to step in and break it.

MAREN: Wow. The way you describe this girl, I might have taken a shot at the other side.

JAIMEY: Yeah. She makes it so easy to love her.

After a while, I'd become knackered so I lied down for a while to rest. Lying flat on my back, the light was bothering my eyes a bit so I decided to close them. Jade and Elaine were still at it and wanted me to continue along with them so they turned the lights off and all we had left was the glare of the digital equipment on my desk. Then . . .

MAREN: What?

JAIMEY: Then . . .

MAREN: And then, what?

JAIMEY: This part's a bit hazy but I know Elaine was still dancing. I'd fallen on the floor at some point and Jade reached down to grab my hand and pull me up. And just as I was getting up . . .

MAREN: Stop pausing! Your smirk's driving me crazy. What?!

JAIMEY: She kissed me.

MAREN: Dear, Lord with that smirk again.

JAIMEY: I'm sorry! I can't help it. It was so unexpected. A bomb blast would have been less surprising.

MAREN: Did you flinch? How did you take it?

JAIMEY: I was transported to an epic romance movie, smack dab on the scene where the hero is carrying his lady in distress after having saved her from the burning building. And that was it. When I pulled out, I looked at her with this feeling of utter panic and awareness, like something inside me had been holding its breath since birth and had finally been taken off its strappings to let the oxygen in.

I had to sit down to take in what had just happened. And when I looked at her . . .

MAREN: Yes?

JAIMEY: It was okay.

In my mind, my thoughts were fighting against each other.

MAREN: What were you thinking?

JAIMEY: I was thinking to push her away. I'd just gotten over the whole struggle with Chris and before, during, and after him, there were some other annoying and obsessive dudes that I'd been busily trying to ward off. But then again, when I looked at her face . . . looking at me . . . it was like . . .

MAREN: Like what?

JAIMEY: I . . .

MAREN: What's the first word that comes to mind?

JAIMEY: Sanctuary.

Chapter 7

I was struggling. My mind was immersed in this great fear that this book will be in Jade's hands someday. And not just hers; my family and friends would also read it. And what, then? My parents would definitely disown me. I don't think I'd ever be able to show my face to them after having opened up their lives for the entire world to see. As their only child, I'd already abandoned them by moving out. Doing this with Maren was like putting salt on their opened wounds.

But it was too late to turn back. I'd already said too much and Maren and I had already signed a contract with the publishers.

MAREN: You saw a sanctuary in her. So you felt protected and at peace, maybe?

JAIMEY: I saw her come out of her reluctant shell that night. Perhaps it had something to do with the alcohol. But when I looked at her, it was as if she was in a deep conversation with my soul and she was speaking to it in the way that I speak to strangers-like long-time friends.

Elaine was still dancing and talking with us but I somehow landed back on the floor. She was on the edge of the bed looking down at me and playing with my hand. We didn't speak to each other but I know that there was some type of communication going on.

MAREN: I bet.

JAIMEY: Maren, do you think we could change the names of the characters in the book and keep me anonymous, somehow?

MAREN: If you like, I suppose that can be done.

JAIMEY: It's just that, I don't know if I'm courageous enough to put my life on a shelf like that.

MAREN: I think you are. But if you want, we can talk about that when the manuscript is finished.

JAIMEY: Okay.

MAREN: So back to your story.

JAIMEY: Yes, well I used to go to London for week long vacations before moving there. I told my parents that they were business trips so that they'd let me go. One year, I met a girl who I'd immediately hit it off with. We spent that week, literally in her flat having wild passionate sex.

                Wait . . . I should take the word, 'passionate,' back.

MAREN: Why?

JAIMEY: I used it in describing Jade. What I had with this girl meant nothing except that I wanted to get it out of my system. At that time, I thought that I was going through a phase-like a temporary craving for something savory or sweet. I remember telling myself that night to get rid of my inhibitions and to accept her invite back to her flat. I thought that once I'd gone through it, I'll start thinking normally again.

        I guess my insistence in following my own set paths were so strong that even my consciousness kept its feelings hidden from me.

MAREN: And in seeing Jade, it felt safe enough to let go.

JAIMEY: Yes. Jade's actions, her speech and even her voice when saying them, and the way she conducted herself with people made her the embodiment of freedom to me.

MAREN: Did you guys get together that night?

JAIMEY: No. But as she stood up to follow Elaine out the door, I grabbed her hand and pulled her back towards me on the bed.

MAREN: But you didn't have sex.

JAIMEY: No. I wanted to though! Believe me. Not just because I was turned on. I'd allotted myself that night to get it done and over with like that other girl. But she stopped me and we fell asleep with our legs and arms intertwined.

MAREN: Intertwined?

JAIMEY: Yeah, like the left and right parts of a pretzel. I don't know how it got that way but we're both very flexible people and especially with alcohol, the extent to our bendability shot to kingdom come.

It scared me, when I woke up in the middle of the night. I panicked and detangled myself away from her. And every other hour after the alcohol had worn out, I'd wake up to try and figure out what had happened and how in hell I'd be able to get out of it.

MAREN: Why were you pushing it away?

JAIMEY: I was petrified beyond belief. Not having sex meant that I couldn't brush away what had happened that night. Alcohol induced or not, this business of attraction was on the table. It would have been easier with a guy because then I could just use eccentricity as my excuse to ignoring it. But I knew ignorance was not an option. We both had the eccentric card and this time, regardless of whether or not the feeling was mutual, I liked her. It had always been the other way around.

And it had always been with men. I didn't know what to do.

MAREN: It sounds like you didn't get any sleep that night.

JAIMEY: After the couple of hours it needed for the alcohol to run its course, I was wide awake. To calm my mind, I even went to my journal and started on a poem about that subject. I was a mess. I didn't know what I was doing.

MAREN: Did you guys talk about it the next morning?

JAIMEY: Great question. We talked the next morning but not about that. That morning marked the beginning of the most memorable of mornings that followed during that summer. Our connection was sealed through our conversations.

It was during mornings such as these that I discovered a great deal about her and as time went on, a great sadness. There was something back home that she was trying to get away from.

She never really touched on those issues though. She'd regale me only with the beautiful things and her great family and friends.

It really wasn't even what she said; it was how she said them that had gotten me hooked. The words in her mind were pushing to get out. And that phenomenon of internal combustion made the tone of her voice sound like music from an orchestra. She was singing her song to me in the rhythm of her own life's composition.

MAREN: You're such a poet.

JAIMEY: I can't help it. She was so new. She was so beautiful.

MAREN: But she never talked about her issues.

JAIMEY: Some, yes-poverty and the pressures of expectations from her family. It was also during that time that I came to learn about her ex. And she went into such great detail that I had the feeling that she still wasn't over him.

MAREN: This was the sadness about her that you mentioned.

JAIMEY: I'm guessing it was a part of it. She made sure that I knew that it was over and even asked if I felt comfortable in listening to her talk about him. It was so early into the relationship yet and I didn't even know whether to call it a relationship. Although the chemistry was apparent, we hadn't spoken about that night and the deeper and the more we got into our talks, the more she made me feel like it was okay.

Plus, I didn't know how to deal with us. If I was to get into a relationship with her, I didn't know what role I'd be playing. I was gushing enough to be the girl but was eager enough to be the guy.

MAREN: Eager?

JAIMEY: I'd never been so excited to share my world with anyone before. I wanted to take her everywhere in Europe and to be the person who showed her, London. Not just London, my London-the city that had brought me so much. I was like Lazarus and the city, my savior.

MAREN: What was it about London? Why, in all of the other cities in the world did you pick this one?

JAIMEY: America is England's lovechild. Most of my favorite writers and authors were from there. And I loved the Victorian setting, both in literature and architecture. My cousin used to live in London and she'd tell me awesome stories about it. The first children's book I read was The Belvidere Rabbit. Over time, my obsession turned into an objective. It changed into a dream of visiting there, and once that was done, of relocating. During the weeks that I'd spent there in the past, I was free to do whatever it was that made me happy. London gave me the right to live.

And Jade to me, was a blank canvas when it came to Europe. I wanted to paint the pictures responsible for bringing my soul to life all over her.

She wasn't though.

MAREN: She wasn't a blank canvas?

JAIMEY: No. She was fluent in French and her obsession for Paris was comparable to mine with London. That was also another thing about her that I loved. Her excitement matched mine to the nth degree. She reflected it.

MAREN: But how did you really feel when she spoke about her ex?

JAIMEY: Beaten. But I wanted to know who he was and what drew her to him.

MAREN: Did you find out?

JAIMEY: I guess it was his ideas and his writing. And . . .

MAREN: And, what?

JAIMEY: Well he was the epiphany of the Gods of attraction to her. He was a hotty! I even agreed to that when I saw his picture.

MAREN: Why did they break up?

JAIMEY: He was a jerk. I hated him for this. He was being brought up . . . . as . . . . something-I don't remember. I just know that his family was expecting him to marry some girl with the same background and he didn't have the balls to go against them.

He used her a lot too. He made her edit his work because . . . I don't know, he lacked grammar? Fuck it. Fuck him. I wanna twist his balls off.

MAREN: One would think that their breaking up would make a great opportunity for you.

JAIMEY: You're right. It did make way for a chance at her. But she was hurt. And over time, it became apparent that she was still in love with him. When I realized the extent to that however, it was too late for me. I'd already fallen for her.

Still, if I had the chance to open that bastard's eyes to what he was really missing by leaving her, I would have.

MAREN: Why?

JAIMEY: I wanted to make her happy-with me or without me.

MAREN: How do you mean by being too late though? The fact remained that they were no longer together.

JAIMEY: She was still talking to him. He said he'd meet her in Paris.

MAREN: How do you know this?

JAIMEY: She told Elaine when we were waiting at the bus stop on our way to the London Zoo. And she'd shared with us one morning in the train to Brighton that he said he loved her.

MAREN: You're so concise with the locations.

JAIMEY: Like I told you, I can give you an exact account of everything that was going on in the moments they happened.

MAREN: But you were talking about-

JAIMEY: I was talking about bad memories-the past. How they never leave you so you just learn to live with them. But that wasn't why I said that it was too late. This happened later.

What I meant was that I'd made a lot of mistakes in approaching this sort of friendship. That's what it was. That's what I should have called it. She needed a friend. I should have treated it that way.

But what I'd seen in her was so mesmerizing that I couldn't help myself. And so, being in the business of trying to achieve everything that I'd ever wanted in life, I sought out to get her, in the same way that I'd sought freedom. The problem was that I didn't know how to show affection. What I was feeling . . . this attraction, it was raw. I was unnerved by it. I was scared.

Still, I emptied myself and let go of everything to make way for this. I was humbled down to my lowest common denominator.

MAREN: Why?

JAIMEY: I wanted to know love in its purest form. To do this, I needed to know nothing of anything else. And in doing this, I saw Europe through new eyes with her, regardless of whether or not I'd been there before. We went to plays, clubs, pubs, little towns, different countries, everything. Doing this with her brought the excitement of life to a higher level.

MAREN: But you were scared.

JAIMEY: Beyond belief. That's why in everything I took her to, I brought Elaine with me. I was . . . I am afraid of being with her alone.

MAREN: Interesting.

JAIMEY: I remember our second morning together-we walked to the café around the corner and ordered our breakfast to go for a picnic in the park across our flat. A couple of people were there but they were soon gone and we had the park all to ourselves. She told me stories of how her mom was like back home-how we had a common love for cooking for the community and how people would smell the scent of her dishes from down the street and go over her house to have a meal with them. It was a beautiful summer day but the grass was too wet to sit on so we ate on one of the two benches that were set up towards the middle of the field that overlooked the entire park. I was hungry and had one or two bites of my English breakfast but I couldn't really eat.

MAREN: Why not?

JAIMEY: I wanted to hold her. I wanted to feel her.

MAREN: Why didn't you?

JAIMEY: I was afraid to. I didn't know how.

I remember that something had landed on my hair and she told me to come closer to her without saying why. Her entire upper body moved gracefully towards me as her left arm reached out to take off whatever it was on my head. And I was frozen. Time had stood still for me to study each of her movements. From that time on, I'd slowly spiraled into this anxious state of silence whenever I was around her-a feeling of anxiety that to this day, I still feel whenever I'm left alone with her.

MAREN: You should have snuck a kiss in there.

JAIMEY: I should have done a lot of things. But from that time on, I started to put a distance between us.

MAREN: How?

JAIMEY: The conversation went to performing arts. We were talking about her love for sewing and I'd suggested that she took a shot at costume designs for plays and what not. The subject went into the Musicals and seeing that she'd never seen a show in London before, I invited her to watch 'Phantom of the Opera,' with me. I took a picture in my mind and framed the look on her face in my memories after I said that. It was fantastic. It was . . . enough.

MAREN: Enough-as opposed to holding her.

JAIMEY: I made her happy. I was satisfied.

I wanted it to be just me and her but I panicked in the end and invited Elaine to come along. I got the wrong tickets but the night went really well. The ladies seemed to have enjoyed it and I was relieved to have Elaine with us so from that time on, I never went anywhere without having her come along.

MAREN: Okay, so I don't get it. Were you guys an item?

JAIMEY: I think it was in the beginning of her second week in London when she told me.

MAREN: There's that smirk again.

JAIMEY: It was weird. Even now, when she messages me starting with the question, "Can I tell you something and you not get mad?" I already know that it's going to be about me, and that it's going to be a confession . . . and it's going to be good.

MAREN: She messaged you this?

JAIMEY: Yes, she lived in the upstairs flats, thank God or I'd never get any work done.

She began with that sentence and after I said that it was okay, she confessed that she'd told a girl that she was into me and that somehow the entire flat had found out about it.

MAREN: How did you react to them knowing?

JAIMEY: I didn't care. And I think she knew that I wouldn't. It was just a way to ease her own anxiety towards the real point of what she was telling me. I loved it! And it was done in a way in which I could take it on-she wrote it to me. Were it done in person, I would never have been able to handle the situation as well as I have.

You see, she also expressed concern about the little time that she had there. In four weeks, she'd have to leave for Paris and five weeks after-back to the states.

MAREN: How did you handle that?

JAIMEY: Distance never mattered to me. Neither did time. I'd become a convert to love. I was its newest disciple. I would have made it work.

It was too early to love her yet but I could feel it coming. It's like hearing someone's footsteps in an empty hall with echoes. It was only a matter of time. And I was prepared to stop at nothing for it to happen. Paris was only a two hour train ride away. I could have and wholeheartedly would have gone there to visit her any time she needed. And after that, well-I figured we'd cross that bridge when we came to it. In any case, I loved airports. My mom used to work there and dad and I used to pick her up from work every night.

When they couldn't afford a babysitter, she'd often bring me to work with her. I'd spend weeks roaming around the terminals-I grew up around travelers. The happiest part of my childhood was molded by the employees that worked there. They knew me by my first name and would bring me food and chat with me during their breaks. The security guards at the gates had even granted me full access to the boarding terminals. Going to the airport was like visiting home.

MAREN: What did she say when you told her this?

JAIMEY: She asked if she could come down. And again, this overwhelming panic set in. My mind was stuttering for words that came out in meager little sentences to her. I didn't know how to act.

MAREN: What's up with that?

JAIMEY: What?

MAREN: You spoke with such confidence and drive when you were messaging her. It brought her to your flat. Why was it that when she was around you, you got scared?

JAIMEY: I still can't explain it. And I blame it for being a big part of the reason for that burgeoning distance between us.

It got so bad that whenever we'd go to social gatherings together, I'd end up talking to other people . . . other guys. And I believe that it was because of it that she started doing the same.

I never did anything with them. Well, except dance provocatively and let them kiss me.

MAREN: What? With her around? That's so wrong.

JAIMEY: I went mad with my inability to show my affection towards her. All it took was for someone to speak to her and I'd get jealous. It was so simple. It was a natural act between two people regardless of their beliefs and stances. It was just talking, for God's sake and I couldn't even do that, let alone do anything else.

MAREN: How frustrating. Is that how it ended?

JAIMEY: No. It ended earlier. That day, I decided to join her and Elaine on the Beatles tour. It wasn't long after we'd all gotten bored of it so I took them to Leicester Square. We had a great time. She liked to eat sushi so we went to have dinner in Chinatown at my favorite sushi place. I was drenched in red bull and alcohol so I was a bit more outgoing than my usual self. It was that night that I finally summed up enough courage to kiss her.

MAREN: And in public too! Well done!

JAIMEY: Not only that, perhaps more importantly than the kiss I also managed to talk to her in the way that I'd always wanted to do.

MAREN: What did you say?

JAIMEY: I told her that she was beautiful. And that if I'd ended up kissing her that night, she shouldn't blame me for not warning her.

MAREN: Whoa! What a bold move. How did she react?

JAIMEY: Entranced . . . . If I do say so, myself.

MAREN: I'm beginning to like your smirks.

JAIMEY: She looked breathtaking when I said it. She didn't know what to say but after a moment of just smiling and immersing ourselves in each other's intense presence, she told me that I made her mouth water.

MAREN: Score!

JAIMEY: Yes! If only she knew the wall I'd broken through for that reaction. I was on a roll and the sensation was strong enough that I could have kept going forever.

MAREN: But that was the day that it ended?

JAIMEY: Yes. When we got back home, she went upstairs and I went to my room. I didn't want it to end. I was feeling so empowered. So I changed into my shorts and went upstairs to knock on her door.

When she opened it, she didn't let me in. Instead, she came outside and closed the door behind her so that no one would hear. And in that empty hallway at around 3:30 in the morning, it all ended.

MAREN: What did she say?

JAIMEY: She was in tears. That's what I mostly remember. Those tears put me in battle mode-much like how Chris was when he saw me trying to hide my own pain after finding out that the Hospital was no longer there.

She started off with that whole distance and time reason, which I quickly shrugged off as nothing I wouldn't be able to handle. I was indestructible. I was prepared for anything that she could have thrown at me. That is until she brought up her family.

MAREN: What about them?

JAIMEY: She said that I was too good of a person to keep leading me on like she had but that she had her family to think about. She couldn't tell them about this and what's more, she was expected to get married once she'd returned home. She said that it was one of the reasons why she moved there. To find someone . . . or something-it got blurry after that.

After listening to her, I knew that I couldn't stand in her way. I knew how much she loved her family. Plus, who was I to stop her from making these choices? My parents didn't know about my sexuality. At that point, I probably wouldn't have been able to tell them either.

And those tears, man. That was too much. I knew that I couldn't compete with the cards that she'd shoved on the table and that I was powerless to stop her crying. So I let her win and went back downstairs.

Elaine was in the hallway on her way back from the kitchen. Distraught was written all over my face so she asked me what was wrong.

That's all it took. The pent up frustrations that had been battling my love for Jade had finally taken its last push and burst out of my mouth in Tongues. I don't know what else I was saying but I kept repeating to Elaine that Jade was crying. I couldn't bear to see her crying. Not her. Not my girl.

And then time stopped again.

MAREN: What do you mean?

JAIMEY: It had to make sure that I heard and understood exactly what Elaine was about to say to me.

MAREN: What did she say?

JAIMEY: "But, Jaimey-that's the thing. She's not your girl."

MAREN: Ouch.

JAIMEY: Elaine told me to go to her room if I needed to talk but I said thank you and went to my own room. I couldn't speak. I needed to write. I needed to straighten out my mind from all these thoughts that it had been bombarded with. But when I finally settled down on my desk to put pen to paper, I had nothing. I was numb for a few of days.

I remember one night when she came down to invite me for bowling with some of her flat mates but I rejected the offer. I couldn't handle being around her. She said that she didn't want to stop being friends with me and that she'd consider it as a big loss if that ever happened.

MAREN: What did you say?

JAIMEY: I felt the same way. But I couldn't do this yet. I needed time for myself. So, I bullshitted the fact that I had to catch up on some work and that I'd join them another time.

That was the night that I finally broke down.

MAREN: What happened?

JAIMEY: I was planning on writing. I needed to write or I knew I'd go insane. My thoughts came in never ending pits and it was affecting my daily routines. I couldn't eat. I couldn't do anything but stay in my room. I mean, what did she mean by leading me on? Was she just having some reckless fun with me? And if so, how could I have been stupid enough to fall for her words in those conversations we'd had that I so devotedly deemed as reverent?

But then again, she was crying. That's something you can't act out so easily.

But then again, maybe those tears were perhaps out of the guilt she'd felt from leading me on.

I didn't get it. I didn't want to get it.

In writing, I thought I'd be able to make sense of it or at least make some peace with it, however temporal it may have been.

MAREN: Were you able to?

JAIMEY: I had nothing. I couldn't write a word. And at the discovery of this inability, I ran to Elaine's room. I didn't even wait for her to say anything. I couldn't hold the tears in any longer. Poor Elaine didn't know what to do.

MAREN: You poor thing. How did you manage to get past it?

JAIMEY: I didn't. I told you. Once love, that's it. I comforted myself in my veneration towards it. So *in vez de mi amor, amor*-In place of my love, love.

After some struggle, I decided to stay friends with her. I had to. Maybe I was hoping that she could see her way through her situation-I don't know. All I know was that I needed to be around her.

That began the nightly loosening of our hellacious behavior around each other.

MAREN: What do you mean?

JAIMEY: Every time I'd be left alone with her, awkwardness set in. My anxiety came back. I was still bent on expressing myself, however. But this time in a way that wouldn't make it seem like I still carried strong feelings for her.

MAREN: That sounds complicated.

JAIMEY: Like you wouldn't believe. The only way that I could get the reaction from her was if we were going somewhere.

MAREN: The reaction? What do you mean?

JAIMEY: I loved making her happy. I can't even begin to describe to you the sensation that would come over me each time she expressed pleasure. And in bringing her to these places, I found solace in the thought that it was because of me.

My defining moment happened in Paris when Elaine and I went to visit her.

MAREN: Hang on. Go back a bit. What did you mean by hellacious behavior?

JAIMEY: The jealousy was still there. Our relationship had gotten positively violent because of it. I was frustrated because I couldn't get over this fear.

MAREN: How did it get violent?

JAIMEY: Out of meaningless disagreements. I don't even remember them but they would explode in all out battles just to prove a worthless point. It was like clockwork. And in the morning, we'd go through it all over again.

MAREN: And even with that, you went along to visit her to another country?

JAIMEY: I couldn't not go. She'd told me via text how lonely she'd felt in being there. All of that which she was experiencing meant nothing if she couldn't share it.

I understood, completely how she felt. But this was Paris. A place that she'd always dreamed of visiting all her life. I don't know if it was the divine providence of paying forward the experience and blessing of travelling to new places, or the discomfort I felt towards her depression that drove me into going. Perhaps it was both. All I knew was that I had to go and I had to make that weekend with her something rejuvenating.

MAREN: That was your defining moment?

JAIMEY: My defining moment came after the first night. As always, we'd gotten into a violent brawl over something stupid. But the truth was that I'd gotten jealous over some man she was talking to at the bar. We'd just finished watching a show at the Moulin Rouge and I was already drunk from the amount of alcohol that I'd been continuously drinking all day. Nothing good could have come from the events that followed.

I remember being bought drinks from some guy. I wasn't alert enough to make out his face. What I did make out was Jade from across the room-kissing the guy that she'd been talking to. A few moments later, the guy's friend approached me to say that Jade decided to go home with them.

MAREN: Oh man.

JAIMEY: That did it. I don't remember much but little snapshots of what happened after that. Me, pushing the guy I'd been dancing with, Elaine pulling me from standing in the middle of the road, me giving directions to my London flat to the French driver, dismissing the concierge's complement about my having beautiful eyes by saying that they were fake and that I wore contacts, and then getting into a fist fight with Jade.

MAREN: A fist fight?! That bad? I thought she was going with the guy from the bar.

JAIMEY: She didn't. Jade wasn't one to leave us like that.

My test came from the morning that followed. We were supposed to check out in the afternoon but as soon as I woke up, I knew that that wasn't going to happen. So I got up to go downstairs to see if I could extend our reservation for another day.

The room looked like the aftermath of trench warfare and the ladies were sprawled on the bed as if they had been knocked unconscious by a blow of the butt of one of the soldier's guns.

I'd awakened Jade at the sound of my rustling. Elaine was still fast asleep.

MAREN: What happened?

JAIMEY: She called my name. I've come to hate and love when she did that.

MAREN: Why?

JAIMEY: It's rare when she addresses me. She usually never has to. I already know that it's me, she's talking to. And whenever she says it to me it wasn't just a call for attention. It was more like a confirmation and affirmation to my true identity. But that was just me. I put meaning in everything she did.

MAREN: You coin the term, hopeless my dear.

JAIMEY: To a tee.

There was a reason why I took her to see, The Phantom of the Opera. In the play, the cast of the show had a Masquerade ball in which they did a number that's lyrics summarized a large part of my life back home.

Masquerade, people's faces on parade. Masquerade-hide your face so the world will never find you.

When she said my name, she spoke to and through the old facades. It was calling for a conversation to my soul-to speak to her, only in the language of truths.

MAREN: All that to a name? Jesus, you got it bad.

JAIMEY: You asked. And shut up. I know I'm smirking.

MAREN: No comment. Go on.

JAIMEY: She called me back to bed. It was in a tone that I haven't heard her speak in for a long time. But I said no and that I had to take care of some business downstairs.

The entire time, I was dreading going back up. I was still a bit upset about what had happened the night before but I didn't want to explain myself because I knew that I had no right to be. By the time I got to the door though, all resentment had passed over and I began to miss her again. We would still have the entire day but the thought of leaving her loomed over my head like the swarming of dark clouds on a windy day.

Elaine was still asleep but Jade heard me come in.

"Come back to bed," she said.

I replied to her-reluctantly: "In a second."

I was nervous to go near her. I took my time in the bathroom; wiping my makeup from last night, brushing my teeth and washing my face. And when there was nothing left to do, I walked towards the bed.

She felt me coming and pulled the covers aside to let me in.

I ugh, I'm sorry but I wonder if they let us smoke here. We're outside but sometimes they still won't let us do it.

MAREN: Go ahead. If it's not allowed, someone will come out to tell us.

JAIMEY: Yeah. Thanks.

MAREN: Sure.

JAIMEY: I lied down facing her as she brought the blanket over me. At that, she left her hand over my waist and brought herself closer. I don't know if we hugged out of remorse for what had occurred or if it was for something more.

I'm struggling to remember what she said to me. Fuck. I really hate myself for this.

MAREN: It's okay-

JAIMEY: No, it's not. It's not. It really isn't. I should remember it. Fuck! I should know this.

MAREN: Do you remember anything she said?

JAIMEY: It was something along the lines of I'm glad you came or I'm sorry or both. I don't-I don't know! Ah! Fuck.

MAREN: Tissue?

JAIMEY: Ugh! I'm sorry, yes please. Thank you. Forgive me. This is crazy.

MAREN: No it's not. You told me. This was too soon to talk about.

JAIMEY: I remember us just holding each other. I remember . . . let's see . . .

I remember breathing really hard . . . it was very heavy breathing. My chest was heavy. Or I could have just imagined it. I don't know but I remember feeling this huge like, burden like, weight lifting off of me. Just by her holding me in silence like that.

MAREN: What was on your mind?

JAIMEY: I wanted to tell her how much I've missed her. Not just since she left for Paris but since that night when she told me that she couldn't be with me any longer. I wanted to apologize for being such an asshole to her for no reason. I wanted . . . ugh! I knew I wanted to tell her everything but I couldn't because there weren't enough variations in my vocabulary to tell her how much I'd been . . .

MAREN: It's okay. Take your time.

JAIMEY: There wasn't enough. There weren't enough words to tell her how much.

MAREN: How much . . .

JAIMEY: It . . . hurt. Ugh, may I have another tissue?

MAREN: Sure.

JAIMEY: I couldn't say everything so I didn't say anything. But her arms around me gave me the feeling that I didn't need to. I was relieved by it.

Soon after, Elaine woke up. She turned her head around and saw us holding each other and turned it back.

"You people are nuts," she said.

MAREN: Yes, poor Elaine!

JAIMEY: That cracked us up. Jade got up to grab her camera and stood on the bed in her underwear to take a picture of me and Elaine still half asleep. I felt a sharp pain when Jade nudged my leg so I sat up to look at it.

"Oh man," I cried in disappointment.

Elaine sat up to see a huge bruise on my outer thigh and abruptly went back down again.

"I'm not surprised. 'Shit right there's Jade. You're both nuts. I had to pry both of you apart before you passed out. I was so stressed; I had to take a long bath to calm myself down."

Jade and I looked at each other and laughed.

> After a second, Elaine stood up and walked to the bathroom and a few minutes later, the sound of water rumbling against the Jacuzzi floor filled the room. Jade, after sharing a bottle of red wine with me suggested that we all get into the tub.

MAREN: That's a rather unusual breakfast.

JAIMEY: She handed it to me saying that it'd keep me from a hangover. I didn't have the heart to tell her that I didn't get hangovers. It made me feel special that she was concerned.

MAREN: Aww. So did you guys all get in?

JAIMEY: Yes but after about an hour's worth of peer pressure-mostly from Jade. I tried everything to fight her off. I literally had to push her off of me. I even sat in the closet and pulled the door shut so she wouldn't get in. But the chick was too powerful for me.

> What she didn't know was that I'd been working out since she left so when she jumped on my stomach in the closet, I picked her up, carried her over to the bathtub and dropped her in.

MAREN: Well, that's a rather aggressive tactic.

JAIMEY: They both were dumbfounded-it was awesome! You don't understand. Jade's taller than me and scrawny but she's built like a rock. She probably beat my ass up the night before.

MAREN: I wish I could have seen their faces! What did she say?

JAIMEY: I couldn't really hear because as soon as that body touched the surface, she pulled me in.

MAREN: That's so funny.

JAIMEY: After chatting about what happened the night before, Jade and I caught each other's eyes. Elaine's mp3 player was playing some slow jams and she had her head rested upwards on the edge of the tub.

"Elaine, can you do me the fattest favor?" I asked. "I know you're relaxing but I ran out of dry clothes and I need for you to go down to the concierge and ask about the extension to our reservation. I went downstairs earlier but they asked me to come down later on because they'd been having trouble with their computer."

After some expressed annoyance, she finally gave in and went downstairs.

MAREN: Inspired move. Well done.

JAIMEY: I needed more time alone with her.

MAREN: Did you guys . . .

JAIMEY: I didn't know that I wanted to. I wanted to be with her. That was enough. She was smiling again. And I knew for a fact that this was because of me. That was enough. That made me happy.

"I knew it," I gloated playfully. "You pushed me away, but I knew it."

MAREN: What did she say?

JAIMEY: She looked down at the bubbles disintegrating on the water. "This would have been easier if I didn't like you so much."

MAREN: She said that?

JAIMEY: Yes.

I pushed myself closer to her as our eyes met, feeling the length of her legs along the way and never leaving her gaze. I admit she'd aroused me but as I moved closer I began to see a reflection in her eyes.

MAREN: Was it what you wanted to see?

JAIMEY: Partly. I felt torn. I just wanted her to be happy. I wanted to make her happy.

"It doesn't take much," she answered. I didn't realize that I told her what I was feeling. "All this that you did, it wasn't necessary. You guys could have stayed at my place. The trip, the show, and the expenses that you keep insisting that you pay for here and in London—I hate that you went through all that. I didn't need a Jacuzzi or a suite at a fancy hotel. I would have been fine standing in the shower with you. I would have been fine with a pale of water and some soap."

I knew that she'd been uncomfortable with me buying things for her. But it never really was for her. What I couldn't bring myself to express verbally or physically, I expressed in giving her these things.

"Right now-right at this moment," I said, "Tell me what you want. Tell me anything you want from me. Tell me what you want me to do. I just want to make you happy."

She might have sensed the urgency or anxiety in my voice. Perhaps she'd sensed that I wanted to make the best of the little time we had. Elaine was due to come back soon.

MAREN: What did she say?

JAIMEY: She said she wanted me to hold her. And when I did, she started crying in my arms.

The water was warm and I could feel each trickle of her tears run down my back. As she began sobbing, I held her closer to me.

"It's okay," I repeated.

As I held her, I felt this surge of strength take over me and a new and acute awareness of what she really needed from us. I fought to ignore it, even then. But if I couldn't help it, I knew that if only for her, I had to pretend.

MAREN: What was it?

JAIMEY: She needed me to be her friend.

Not long after, Elaine walked in on us. I'd been sitting still—immersed in the moment and trying to get my fill by holding her.

Elaine paused in her tracks, took one look at us and said, "Ya'll need to stop playin'."

We laughed.

MAREN: Poor Elaine.

JAIMEY: Yeah. The things I put that girl through.

Oh, but we had great fun that day. We missed our train ride but we met up with a couple of Jade's friends who gave us a tour of the real Paris-away from the tourist attractions.

That night, all three of us had to share a bunk in Jade's dorm room but I wouldn't have traded it for the world.

I couldn't get to sleep yet though because after the weeks since she dropped the bomb on me on that hallway, I'd finally reclaimed my ability to write. I was a maniac on Jade's keyboard. I even heard her laughing at my frantic typing in the middle of the night when I thought she'd fallen asleep.

Finally at around 4am, I finished writing. I didn't want to squeeze myself on the bed because as it was, the girls were already barely able to move.

But again, and in the same tone I'd heard her use that morning, Jade called me to come to bed.

I smiled and sat on the edge next to her. There was literally about an inch worth of space between her and the edge but she patted the surface and motioned for me to lie down. As I positioned myself sideways, facing away from her, I took her left arm and held it over my waist as I slipped my legs in between hers-one in the middle and one over.

I wanted the perfect ending for one of the most perfect days in my life that night in Paris. I knew she was happy. And I barely even spent a thing.

MAREN: Beautiful.

JAIMEY: It was.

I wish it ended that way.

MAREN: It didn't?

JAIMEY: No. Less than few weeks later, she would return to London for her last weekend stay in Europe. Both she and Elaine would be returning to the states a day later and we'd planned on going to Ibiza. Well, I planned it.

When I got back to my flat from the trip, I was resolute to changing my ways of things when it came to Jade. I was her friend. I had to only be her friend. I'd brushed whatever feelings I had aside and decided to play the role. But as the days to her departure got closer, I panicked. So instead of wallowing in heartbreak for the day, I thought it'd be perfect if we could squeeze in another trip and spend that time exploring. I denied it at one point but I secretly knew that she wanted to visit Ibiza. Again, I was back at it with my relentless mission to keep her smiling. However indirect or misguided it may have been, I needed this outlet to express my true feelings for her.

That weekend or so before, I'd arranged for us to meet in Spain with three of my friends. I missed her so much. But once there, I'd managed to go through completely without showing any signs of affection towards her. But that only fueled my angst towards the impending event of her leaving. I still had school and the U.S. wasn't a two hour train ride away. Had I even done that, it would have been impossible to cover it up with the façade of friendship. This sort of thing would have been an act of love-an area that I'd long since been banned from.

MAREN: Sounds like you banned yourself though, in a sacrificial act.

JAIMEY: It's what I saw that she needed.

MAREN: Yes, I understand.

I wonder—did that guy ever make it to Europe?

JAIMEY: Ah, the ghost opponent-no. She didn't seem surprised, though. She'd said to us the day Elaine asked about him that it was normal for people to say things that they don't follow through on. It sounded like she was used to it. That son of a bitch. She made it sound blasé, but I saw through it. She was broken.

MAREN: I'm glad he didn't go. Dear, what a pain it is to have to fight a ghost. You can't. You'd always lose.

JAIMEY: I'd learned that fact very well, indeed.

MAREN: So what happened that last weekend? How did Ibiza go?

JAIMEY: It didn't. The night she came back, we started drinking recklessly. It was the weekend she met Chris. It was also the night that she found out that I'd been with him while she was in Paris.

What she didn't know was that this whole thing happened before our visit there and that I'd done it in a feeble attempt to get over her.

MAREN: Why didn't you tell her?

JAIMEY: I was feeling the time drawing near. I wanted to make like I was okay with things being as they were. I did want to tell her but my mind was telling me not to. Why would it have mattered if we were only friends?

So I kept drinking and kept trying to ignore her. The argument that night was sparked by it. She followed me into my room because she'd left some things there before leaving for Paris. It was there that she expressed her concern towards my drinking and I snapped. I was so stupid. After that, all hell broke loose. The argument that had ensued was over something so petty that I can't even recall it. But I remember being so angry that I'd finished over a half a bottle of whiskey before passing out.

The next morning, when I went to Elaine's room to wake the girls up for our trip, she said she didn't want to go.

I was so angry that I'd returned to my room and smashed the crap out of my guitar. Besides writing, playing the guitar had always brought me peace from the chaos of the world around me.

But I didn't care and I didn't stop until all that was left was the handle.

I remember downing another full bottle of wine that morning and seven more during day starting from the moment I woke up.

MAREN: How did she handle that?

JAIMEY: Jade? She slept through the day and well into the afternoon. On top of the wine she'd had, I know that she soloed an entire large bottle of Jack Daniels.

MAREN: Christ.

JAIMEY: When she woke up, Elaine told her what had happened the night before and what I did to my guitar. I'd overheard her talking through the walls of our bedrooms. Almost immediately after their conversation, she walked fervently to my room and stopped at the disastrous mess I'd created of what was once a musical instrument. It was as if I'd planted a bomb inside it and it blew up from the middle of the room. Wood chips were everywhere.

MAREN: What did she say to you?

JAIMEY: She kept apologizing. At first, it was about Ibiza but then the more she repeated it, the more I felt like she was saying sorry for putting me through what I'd gone through since we'd met.

I hated that she did that but while she was sleeping, I'd managed to put on my mask in preparation for the final masquerade that I'd RSVP'd to when I first realized my feelings for her. The official ball would begin when she'd finally awaken.

MAREN: How did you manage to do that? You must have been a complete and utter mess.

JAIMEY: I wrote her a letter, spilling my guts out to her. I ripped out the pages from my very first journal. That journal was hand sown with a brown leather cover, so outdone that I could imagine the animal it had once belonged to. I bought it after saving up for months when I first started writing. It was my first gift to myself and over the years had become the resting place for my soul.

MAREN: Did she know that?

JAIMEY: She probably didn't even know that she had the letter until she unpacked back home.

MAREN: Why did you do it?

JAIMEY: My journey, this whole moving business and finding my way in the world had culminated with her. I knew that there couldn't be anything more important than that world-shattering feeling I had when I first looked into her eyes. What I'd written that far-my new adventures and discoveries—I'd already recorded. Whatever happened afterwards would have just been a cliché. Unfortunately, fate had chosen her to show this stranger to me-this.. thing . . . this . . . Love. Perhaps I should have been the one to say sorry that she was used as a tool.

MAREN: Did you?

JAIMEY: I don't know that I did. I was too preoccupied about what she was telling me at the time.

MAREN: What did she tell you?

JAIMEY: She told me that she was tired. She said that she wanted to go home. She was grateful for everything that she'd experienced in coming here but that she missed her family and friends. Again, she was so sorry about Ibiza but she couldn't understand why I was in such a hurry to do everything.

MAREN: What did you say?

JAIMEY: I told her that I was afraid I'd never see her again. I had a tendency of going off without telling anyone where I was going. Besides a couple of friends, I'd never come across anyone who'd give a damn. What's more, I had the habit of being alone and secluding myself from societal routines.

While that was the truth, I was referring to the darkest moments of my past. I knew I wasn't the same anymore. I knew that, that wouldn't be the reason why I wouldn't see her again. Remember,

I was in character in the middle of a masquerade ball.

MAREN: What was the real reason?

JAIMEY: I couldn't bear her. I couldn't bear that mask. I'd worn it a few times when I was with her and it failed me. Even before Paris, when I had a weaker resolution. It was so unsuccessful that one night I even professed my love to her only to be shut down. She was so upset that she'd locked the doors to her room and wouldn't even answer with me knocking frantically at it.

MAREN: That sounds like one of the stories you'd told me with Chris.

JAIMEY: Yeah. A close friend of mine, Cocoa pointed that out to me. I am the uncanny female version of Chris.

MAREN: And again with the strange connections. Your life, I tell you.

Anyway, what else did she say in the room?

JAIMEY: She asked me if I was dying. A flashback of my last meeting with my doctor zoomed through my mind as I was taken aback with her question. Perhaps she was right. It made a lot of sense. I never allowed myself to react to the news of the possibility.

MAREN: But how did she find out?

JAIMEY: My glands were swollen. They still are now. They're the permanent reminders of my unhealthy past. I'd been used to my body swelling up from my past excursions to the hospital. I remember one time when they kept me on strict supervision for three weeks at the intensive care unit and my entire body had swelled up to double its size.

MAREN: Geez, why?

JAIMEY: The lining between my blood stream and the skin which held proteins had dried up. Proteins absorb the water to keep from swelling up when we retain them. Since I was dehydrated, they pumped me with all kinds of liquid electrolytes. But since I was also malnourished and lacked the proteins that I needed, I swelled like a balloon. What added to it were my kidneys. Before that last doctor's visit, the blood test had always shown that they were deficient in some way. That's also why I bruised so easily.

MAREN: How did she react to this?

JAIMEY: I don't recall her having any. She told me to slow it down and to take time to absorb everything that was happening. It was a bit upsetting because that was what I came to London for-to absorb.

It frustrated me and caused me to tear up a little but I was unyielding. I had to keep the high spirited front up for as long as I could.

She'd been trying to spend as much time with me as she could. She tried to get me to dinner with her but by the time she was fully awake, all of the shops had been closed. So I ordered delivery from a late night sushi shop and invited everyone to our kitchen for a farewell get together.

I kept trying to ignore her. I'd sneak glances here and there but I was always careful to make sure that she was looking the other way so as to not risk meeting eye to eye.

At one point, I felt her watching me but I didn't turn. But as if she knew that I was aware of what she was doing, she said, 'If you cut me off from Facebook, I'm coming to New York to hunt you down—you hear me?'

I smiled. But then someone brought up Chris again and that I think was the beginning of the war to end all wars.

MAREN: World War One.

JAIMEY: Yes but a successful version of it. This actually ended it.

Chapter 8

We didn't realize that it would take such a long time for Jade's story to end. Maren's husband had been looking for her for hours. There were over a dozen missed calls and around 10 or 12 messages by the time she'd realized that her phone was turned off. We had no choice but to schedule another session.

MAREN: I'm sorry I had to go last night. The hubby was going insane with worry.

JAIMEY: It's not a problem. I totally understand. I hope it went okay.

MAREN: Yes, yes. I had to calm him down a bit but all was well.

JAIMEY: Good. I'm glad.

MAREN: Now where were we? Ah yes—WWI-the war to end all wars.

JAIMEY: Yes. Maybe it should have been called The Cold War though. It put an embargo on all forms of communication with Jade for a long time.

MAREN: Go on.

JAIMEY: There'd been a party going on in the student commons and the lot of us decided to go.

We were in and out of the kitchen between my flat and the courtyard. I could tell that I'd made her upset when we came back in.

Chris walked into the courtyard when were gathered there. Elaine made the introduction but they didn't speak to each other-not even as much as a greeting.

As my group was walking back inside, Chris called for me to wait for a second when I got to the door. He'd been in a state of confusion as to what happened the night we had sex. I never spoke to him again in the days that followed, I didn't blame him. As I held on to the door, he moved to within a breathing distance towards me.

Jade saw this as she was entering my flat and held the door to call my name in that familiar tone. I turned towards her but I was stopped by an instant reminder of the mask I was meant to be wearing.

"In a sec," I said as I looked back towards Chris with a smirk.

She gave a sound of exhalation as she shut the door behind her.

Chris bent over to kiss me but I stopped him.

"I gotta go," I said.

This got to him. He demanded a talk with me but my mind was elsewhere and I couldn't deal with it. I wanted to return to the kitchen right after her. I needed to make sure that it was quick enough to give her an idea that there wasn't enough time to have done anything with him. Schizophrenic, I know. But I couldn't help it.

MAREN: Did Chris follow you in?

JAIMEY: No. He told me that if I didn't talk to him, that that would be the end of our friendship. That would be the end of us. He didn't talk to me for weeks. He even ignored me when we happened upon each other on the street one day.

MAREN: How did you feel about that?

JAIMEY: Like I might have missed out on what could have been a great friendship. But I was kind of glad at the same time. I didn't want him to love me in that way. I mean, look at what I'd become. I wouldn't wish that on anyone.

MAREN: So you went back to the kitchen immediately after?

JAIMEY: Not Immediate enough.

MAREN: Did Jade look upset?

JAIMEY: I couldn't bring myself to look at her.

Not long after, we all decided to go to the party. It seemed like everyone was there celebrating the end of the term. I didn't stay but a minute. I was tired. I didn't want to keep pretending to be interested in anyone else when I knew that the one person who I wanted to spend time with had been engaged in talking with some Spanish guy I'd met a couple of days before she came back from Paris.

I had to keep my jealousy at bay. So I went outside and hung out with my other flat mate. The guy who was throwing the party was involved in a quarrel with him so he was celebrating outside with some other people.

After less than an hour, we were the only two people left in the courtyard. Derhem was drunk and complaining about Anand again. I wasn't paying attention. I was lost in my jealousy of what might have been happening at the party. And as if the fates had pried open a crack in my brain to let the fears seep through, I saw the door of the student common open and two figures dashing across the courtyard and into the building of my flat.

I excused myself from Derhem. I kept trying to turn myself around back towards the student commons but my feet had taken on a new brain and it kept going. They were in Elaine's room. I heard them as I walked past. And God help the ass hole who built those thin walls because I was desperate to drown out the sounds and drench myself in enough wine to go to sleep.

MAREN: Oh no. What did you do?

JAIMEY: I wanted to punish myself somehow, first off for not being able to control my tears.

Do you mind if I light one?

MAREN: No. There's an ashtray on that table-let me get it for you.

JAIMEY: Thanks

Hey that's a nice ashtray, I wonder if they'll miss it.

MAREN: I don't think so. There's plenty more on the other tables.

JAIMEY: You're my kind of woman.

So anyway, the noise had grown louder. I wasn't sure whether or not it was my imagination. All I know was that I couldn't bring myself look at her again. She'd be leaving in the morning but her things were left in my room. The alcohol had failed me and I was still wide awake.

MAREN: What did you do?

JAIMEY: I wanted to go into the kitchen for another bottle and lock myself in my room in the hopes of sleeping to and through at least the morning. First though, I had to move her things into the hallway so that she wouldn't have to enter.

MAREN: What else was going through your mind?

JAIMEY: Nothing. By that time, I'd managed to calm myself... or rather numb myself from all feeling. I'd been focused on my hat that had somehow gotten lost during the evening. I was wearing it all day. I bought that fedora in Camden market and wore it everywhere I went.

I found Elaine and Derhem sitting in the kitchen, smoking Derhem's shisha.

MAREN: Shisha?

JAIMEY: I'm sorry, hookah.

MAREN: Ah.

JAIMEY: Yeah there are many names for it depending on which country you go to. Derhem's from Yemen, the son of the beverage King. He was known throughout the court for his wild parties and never ending supply of shisha. He was such a lovely guy; I couldn't imagine why Anand hated him.

Anyway, when I saw the two sitting there, I asked Elaine if she'd seen my hat. She said that it was in her room but that she'd have to give it to me in the morning before she left because she couldn't go in there at the moment.

"That's okay, Elaine," I said, "I'll go get it myself."

Elaine looked worried. "Oh, dear. Jaimey, please don't."

MAREN: You went in?

JAIMEY: No. I walked as far as the front door but couldn't bring myself to knock, thank God.

When I went back into the kitchen to get my bottle, I gave Elaine a hug goodbye and said that I wasn't going to be able to see her in the morning.

MAREN: What did she say?

JAIMEY: She said she had to spend the night with me because her room was taken.

MAREN: Poor Elaine.

JAIMEY: Ha-ha yeah. I was gonna miss my personal buffer.

I told her that I'd keep my door unlocked for when she was ready to come in but that during and after she left, I wanted her to keep it locked at all times. It didn't turn out that way though.

I tripped over her slippers on my way to the bathroom early the next morning when I woke up. I could hear Jade outside busily trying to pack her scattered belongings in the hallway,

I waited until it was silent, hoping that she might temporarily leave so I could toss them out. But I misjudged and saw her blur in front of her bag.

MAREN: Blur?

JAIMEY: It had only been barely a couple of hours since I went to sleep after another bottle of red. Blurs were all I could make out at that point. Plus I'd only seen her at the corner of my eye.

I didn't want to say anything so I made sure to drop her slippers loud enough to get her attention.

As I turned back to my room, I heard her say goodbye to me in a strange and small squeak of a tone.

MAREN: Well it was awkward. I don't blame her. Did you say bye back?

JAIMEY: Yes. Firmly towards her, before slamming the door shut and walking to my computer to take her off my friend's list on Facebook.

MAREN: And . . .

JAIMEY: And the End.

MAREN: I know you better than that.

JAIMEY: You're right. The next day, I messaged her on Skype to apologize for my behavior.

MAREN: What did she say?

JAIMEY: She called me a hypocrite and said that it might be good to keep our distance and not talk to each other for a while.

She was right. It gave me a chance to reflect and focus on all the responsibilities that I'd set aside-like my dissertation.

MAREN: Oh man.

JAIMEY: Yeah. It was assigned to us in the beginning of the term but I'd only started the research about a couple of weeks before it was due. Plus, I needed to find a place to stay in New York.

MAREN: How did you get over what happened?

JAIMEY: I didn't. I left it to time to perform this miracle.

At first, I couldn't get myself to do anything. I kept drinking and started smoking. I got fat.

MAREN: Well you're far from it now so I'm guessing you did well enough in handling it.

JAIMEY: Hamlet ones called the whole world a stage. The show had to go on so I made myself act in yet another self-preserving masquerade. I had to pretend that nothing was bothering me for the sake of my beloved audience. Interestingly enough, I'd become a spectator myself. The performer and the viewer, and the speaker and the listener-or the manipulator and the fool of a disastrously relegated play

MAREN: Relegated?

JAIMEY: This final act was not of my own composition. It was the 180 degree turn of the tragedy that had become of it. I didn't want to leave London. Time was fucking me over with the impending due date of the dissertation.

MAREN: And Jade?

JAIMEY: Yeah. Jade. I ate, slept, drank, and breathed every breath with her in my mind. It was to the point where I even inadvertently typed her name on my report.

MAREN: Jaimey, what was so special about this audience that made this masquerade go on? Besides you, who was in it? Jade left.

JAIMEY: Wrong. She in fact, took over entire rows of seats. The rest were my friends, family and professors. I didn't want to speak of the war-torn chaos that I'd made of my consciousness. I had to play a strong character-a leading one . . . a winning one.

It was writing that saved me. I'd stay in my room for days and go out only if I needed supplies from the store. Even then, I'd do this at night when I knew that everyone had gone to their rooms. I had to maintain my character in class so as to not let on to my professors that I'd barely even begun my research. With this I managed to complete in two days-all fifty or so thousand words of my paper just in time to turn it in by the midnight deadline. With this, I managed to get Jade talking to me again. I needed us to be okay for the rest of the masquerade to go on. And once that was taken care of, I was left to focus on the reality of the damages that had taken place in the thought of leaving London and the aftermath of losing Jade; This time, without the mask.

I'd never written so much in my life and the fact that I didn't have an answer made my writing better.

MAREN: You didn't have an answer to what?

JAIMEY: To how my spirit could have so recklessly set itself up for such a great fall. Towards that final month, I'd been left alone to make sense of my demons. And in the process it came to me that

that this wasn't an act of recklessness at all. This whole thing... everything was one big.... giant leap of faith. It was-it is faith. I left my family and livelihood in its name and as a result, I was blessed with my own family of the friends that I'd met along the way. London didn't fail me. It created me.

MAREN: And Jade?

JAIMEY: Maren, my sessions with you was quiet a journey. I'm not sure about the impression I made of Jade but I hope that it was a good one. The masquerades, the pretensions, and even the pursuits I'd made for her were all acts of selfishness. I saw love and thought that I could own it.

MAREN: Did the time without her help you get over your feelings for her?

JAIMEY: A priest from a Sikh temple back in Cali once said, 'Mohabbat, Rab qui meherbani hai.' Love is god's sacrifice. I don't profess to know what love is much like I don't profess to know who God is but I'd learned that they're interchangeable—each one, a gift from each one. Love was God's gift to me. I travelled all over the world because my love was in every one of those places. It was in every one of those places that I learned freedom.

Did I get over my feelings for Jade?

Jade was part of the blessing. In travelling, I found freedom. In Jade, I found love. How can I ever get over that? Meeting her was something so powerful that I ripped the rest of the blank pages of my journal because I believed that there was nothing left to write about.

MAREN: Still, it must have been so painful. My husband was my first boyfriend so I can't imagine how it was for you.

JAIMEY: In love, God. He is by definition and in an acceptable cliché, omnipotent.

No matter what, in whatever form it is, God is good. That hurt I feel, then . . . that too, is good.

After all, He molded me. I believe London was a part of His plan for me. I wouldn't have been published, otherwise.

MAREN: True but you're a human being. Human beings hurt.

JAIMEY: Human beings were designed to do so, yes. It's part of their performance in life-in love. Like I said, it's all one big leap of faith. I've learned not to question the production process any more. I am what love let me become.

CPSIA information can be obtained at www.ICGtesting.com
Printed in the USA
BVOW011325200312

285627BV00001B/23/P